Taking Lily's hand, he pulled her down beside him on a rock. Looking around, Lily noticed that they were on the far side of the lake—still within earshot of the others, but just out of view.

Fog hovered over the water, drifting over them, smudging the night scenery like a glorious wet painting. With a sigh, she let it all surround her—the crickets singing, the branches brushing together in the light breeze, the others talking back at camp…

Her own heartbeat.

Lily looked at him, at his profile with his strong, masculine features and the mouth that she so desperately wanted on hers.

"I want to strip you out of your clothes and take you right here," he growled.

"The others—"

"Can hear, I know. We'll be quiet," he said, his voice sharp with desire.

He looked at her then, his glasses slipping just a little, a frown on his mouth. His jaw was shadowed with stubble and his hair had been finger combed. He was definitely a bad boy. An irresistibly sexy bad boy.

And lucky for Lily, bad boys were her weakness….

Blaze™

Dear Reader,

Writing this series with Stephanie and Jacquie was a fun adventure all in itself. I'm honored to share their readers, and thrilled to open ADRENALINE RUSH with two characters who haven't quite been lucky in their own adventures lately. I do like to torture my people before I give them their happily ever after!

The torturing this time takes place in the mountains. It's not often I go camping. Since I live in the Sierras, I can just look out my windows and see the glory. I don't have to sleep in a sleeping bag on rocky terrain, don't have to wake up to spiders and bugs in my tent.

And it's not often I get to strip down and go skinny-dipping either, but Lily and Jared get to do all that and more. Watching them fall in love amongst the glorious mountain trails I know so well was great fun. Even with a host of quirky characters making things interesting.

I hope it inspires you to find your own ADRENALINE RUSH!

Happy reading,

Jill Shalvis

JILL SHALVIS

Just Try Me...

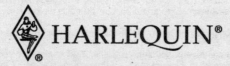

TORONTO • NEW YORK • LONDON
AMSTERDAM • PARIS • SYDNEY • HAMBURG
STOCKHOLM • ATHENS • TOKYO • MILAN • MADRID
PRAGUE • WARSAW • BUDAPEST • AUCKLAND

ISBN-13: 978-0-373-79274-0
ISBN-10:   0-373-79274-3

JUST TRY ME...

This edition published by arrangement with Harlequin Books S.A.

® and TM are trademarks of the publisher. Trademarks indicated with ® are registered in the United States Patent and Trademark Office, the Canadian Trade Marks Office and in other countries.

www.eHarlequin.com

Printed in U.S.A.

ABOUT THE AUTHOR

Jill Shalvis also lives in the Sierras, where she regularly survives hiking expeditions while surrounded by quirky characters. But these characters are her family, and she hardly ever has to dive off cliffs and jump into icy rivers to rescue people. Any other similarities between her life and *Just Try Me...* are purely coincidental.

Look for her bestselling, award-winning novels wherever romances are sold, and check out her Web site at www.jillshalvis.com.

Books by Jill Shalvis
HARLEQUIN BLAZE
63—NAUGHTY BUT NICE
132—BARED
232—ROOM SERVICE

HARLEQUIN TEMPTATION
938—LUKE
962—BACK IN THE BEDROOM
995—SEDUCE ME
1015—FREE FALL

Prologue

WILDLAND FIREFIGHTER Lily Peterson stood on the edge
of a cliff, surrounded by a three-hundred-and-sixty-
degree vista of what should have been glorious Montana
mountains. Instead, the peaks were charred black and
still smoking.

She was on mop-up duty. It meant walking and in-
vestigating every little plume of smoke rising from the
dead mountains; arduous, dirty, exhausting work. She
was at the far end of the burn, standing between devas-
tation and new growth. Her job—protect the unscorched
areas from a flare-up. No easy feat with the earth
beneath her feet still radiating heat.

Both above and below her, the trees were nothing but
skeletons. Hundreds and hundreds of years of forest de-
velopment destroyed because some jerk hadn't put out
his campfire properly.

But they'd saved this part of the forest. It'd taken
weeks. As a result, she was exhausted, right down to the
bone, practically stumbling on her feet with it, but
they'd done good.

The sun was just rising. Eyes gritty from lack of
sleep, Lily patted her pockets for her sunglasses, but

she must have left them back at the barracks. Lifting her head, she shielded her eyes with her hand and looked around for the others. She stepped closer to the edge of the plateau on which she stood, high above the valley by a good hundred feet. Matt and Tony were far below her, at least half a mile away, separated from each other by several football fields, walking east, heads down, doing just as she was.

Watching for flare-ups.

After six straight weeks of firefighting, eating while standing up, grabbing only catnaps when they could, she felt woozy, dead on her feet.

And the sun was killing her.

She turned her back on the valley, and observed the burned area around her. There was so much to keep an eye on, too much. Budgeting and financial cutbacks kept them perpetually understaffed, resulting in too many hours on-site and too few hours off for recuperation, not to mention too few people working at any one time.

When she found herself actually weaving, practically asleep where she stood, she backed up to a tree, slowly sliding down until she sat on the ground, her head resting against the trunk.

She lowered her hand from her face and then couldn't keep her eyes open in the bright glare. So she closed them, just for a moment.

And never saw the new, dark-black plume of smoke rising from a hot spot, only five yards away...

1

LILY LAY FLAT on her back, her physical therapist pushing her leg up over her head as though she were a pretzel, telling her to "work it, Lily, stop whining and work it," while pain seared a fiery line from her ass to the very tip of her hair.

Lily would like to work him, all right—right into a bloody pulp.

Instead she gritted her teeth and told herself that this was the price she paid for stupidity.

No self-pity, she decided as she began to sweat like a stuck pig, her tank top sticking to her skin, her leg quivering wildly as she stretched her abused, injured muscles… Damn, she hurt.

Maybe retiring wasn't so bad. It wasn't as if it was the first time. From high school, she'd gone into expedition guiding, which she'd retired from to become a paramedic. And when she'd burned out scooping stab victims off the streets of Los Angeles, she'd retired again to become a wildland firefighter.

And she'd loved it. Thrived on it, actually, moving from fire to fire, exploring Montana, the Dakotas, Idaho, Wyoming…a perfect fit for her restless spirit.

Until she'd screwed up and nearly gotten herself killed.

Nope, there was no sugarcoating this retirement; she was no longer a firefighter—because of injuries, not by choice. She felt weak and insignificant, and at the age of twenty-nine-and-three-quarters, she wasn't ready for either. She wanted to be back out there, damn it, doing her thing, going where she wished, doing something she loved and was good at.

But she couldn't have passed an agility test to save her life. Hell, she couldn't even touch her toes at the moment.

"Harder, Lily."

She squeezed her eyes shut and stretched harder, feeling her muscles pull and burn. And yet still, beyond the pain, she also felt...itchy. She needed to be on the move, working with adrenaline as her daily friend. It was a pattern in her life, an affliction. It was who she was, what she did.

Or who she'd used to be anyway—a terrifying thought because...who the hell was she now? "Damn it, *ow*," she said to her PT, a gorgeous man who resembled Denzel Washington.

Eric nodded in approval and backed off. "Was wondering if you even had a pain threshold there for a minute."

"Got it, and we hit it."

He smiled—because it wasn't *his* muscles they were torturing. "Wait here. I'm going to get you some ice."

She'd spent a lot of time in and out of the hospital since her Screw-Up. Major, life-threatening injuries did that to a person. But she'd still not learned to be a good waiter. In fact, waiting was for sissies who needed a minute, and she absolutely did not. She had things to do, places to go. Rolling over, she pushed up to her hands and knees, still trembling like a damn newborn.

Or a wildland firefighter who'd woken up in the middle of a full-blown flare-up, forced backwards by the flames, where she'd taken a fall off the cliff, hitting a few burning trees on the way down. Forty feet down. An *ex*-firefighter now, who couldn't move an inch. She collapsed to her belly, and lay there like a beached whale.

Okay, so maybe she did need a minute.

Around her the PT office buzzed with the low hum of voices, the whir of equipment. More people being pushed to the edge of sanity… Someone's cell phone rang. Lily hated cell phones. Truthfully, she wasn't crazy about anything electronic, which she supposed made her an outcast in her own generation.

But give her a wide-open space with nothing marring the sound of a soft breeze any day. Thinking it, yearning, she looked out the window toward the Golden Gate Bridge. Unfortunately, San Francisco didn't have a lot of wide-open spaces. Not the way she liked them anyway, the kind that took three days of walking to get to civilization.

Nearby, something else beeped—someone's Blackberry, or a laptop—and she sighed, missing being outside. The mat beneath her smelled like the sweat and tears of all the previous patients Eric had worked over, and she crawled to one of the chairs lining the wall.

All around her were the injured and the hurting, and it depressed her enough to keep to herself. She scanned the stack of magazines. Fashion, gossip rags…then her gaze snagged on *U.S. Weekly Review,* and the cover article—"Adrenaline Rush."

Huh. Interested in something for the first time in too long, she risked the pain to reach for it. "Ow, ow, ow…" The magazine opened right to the cover article. Beneath the title was a single-line testimonial from the editor of the magazine.

This article changed my life, give it a try!

No article had ever changed Lily's life, and with no small amount of skepticism, she began to read. The author believed life was all about risk-taking, and how too few people actually risked at all, much less lived life to its fullest.

So far, Lily agreed. Hadn't she taken more than a few risks in her life, the latest of which had resulted in her being here right this minute? As for living life to its fullest…well, she'd done that, too. In all areas.

Okay, in all areas except maybe one, but she didn't want to think about her love life.

Or lack thereof. Men tended to come in and out of her world like the passing of a tide, no one having made a lasting impression. She knew what it said about her that she'd never had a real long-term relationship, and she didn't care. Her life wasn't conducive to long-term anyway, including men.

With a sigh, she went back to the article. "Jumpstart your life" it demanded, and went on to explain that a risk didn't have to be physical, it just had to be something off her own beaten path.

Well, since the path she'd been on had been a dizzying whirlwind of doctors and more doctors, she felt more than ready for different, thank you very much.

But how to do it? She was a mere shadow of her former self. How could she ever find the courage to risk again?

But…could she stand not to?

"Ah, here you are," Eric said, returning with the promised icepack. He patted the mat next to him, and with a groan, she tossed the magazine aside and crawled back to work.

Two months later

LILY HAD HEALED just enough to be restless as hell. And frustrated.

And truthfully? *Scared.* It showed in the lingering nightmares of waking up surrounded by flames, it showed in her sudden dislike of being alone.

She could have called her mother, but her mother liked the idea of Lily "settling down," "acting her age." Lily had no siblings, and her father…well let's just say she was entirely too like him.

Or so she'd been told. Since he hadn't been around in years, she couldn't be sure.

It didn't matter. She was alone, and that's just the way it was. But for the first time in her life, she wasn't strong, and she hated that. She needed…something, something to show her she could become the person she'd been before her accident.

But more than that, she needed money. She'd been searching for a viable job for weeks now, and had found nothing to interest her. But funds were running low and the criteria was going to have to change from what interested her to what fed her.

She opened her paper to the want ads and her gaze immediately locked on one in particular. A trek guide was needed ASAP by an expedition company— Outdoor Adventures, to be exact.

Lily stared at the ad and felt a rush of emotion, along with a sense of deja vu. Outdoor Adventures, where she'd first worked as an eighteen-year-old guide, nearly twelve years ago. Jumpstart your life…take a risk… It was like a sign, right? She could start over, back at the beginning. Maybe she could become strong again. Become the person she'd once been.

Without letting herself think, she reached for the phone and called the number listed, though in truth, she somehow still had it memorized. A receptionist answered, and she heard herself ask for Keith Tyler, but when he came on the line with his low, almost unbearably familiar voice, she went still, bombarded by memories: climbing mountains, leading treks, being young and strong and…and nothing like she was now.

"Hello?" Keith said again, a hint of impatience in his tone now. "Anyone there?"

"Wow," she finally managed. "You sound the same."

There was a pause. Then, "Lily? Lily Peterson?"

"How are you, Keith?"

"Thrilled to hear from you. I was just thinking about you not too long ago, wondering if you remembered me."

"Of course I remember. You were…" Would she say her first boss…or her first lover?

Both applied.

He merely chuckled. "Yeah, I always was hard to pi-geon-hole. Still am, to be honest."

Lily lay back on her bed, closed her eyes, and was transported back in time. Having just graduated high school, she'd finally been able to give in to the wander-lust bug. She'd left Los Angeles, her mother and friends, and had gone to work as an expedition guide.

Keith's guide. Ten years her senior, he'd been gor-geously worldly, and of course, sexy as hell. All that long, hot summer, she'd worked for Outdoor Adventures, guiding hiking trips through the Sierras, teaching people about the outdoors by day, and by night…well, Keith had certainly taught her plenty by night, every night.

Until she'd moved on to her next adventure, and left him and all the memories behind.

But not *too* far behind, given the odd *ping* low in her belly just from listening to his voice. "I saw your ad in the paper," she said.

"And I saw you, not in the want ads though, but the front page. You had quite a fall."

After all these months, she still flinched. She hated that her mistake, her failure, had been so public. "Yeah."

"You broke your back. You…you're in a wheelchair now, yes?"

"No."

"But the article said you weren't expected to walk again, that—"

"I'm fine now." If fine meant a stupid limp and some serious lingering aches and pains that made her feel like an old lady all the time.

"But not fine enough to fight fires?"

"And to think, once upon a time, I loved your characteristically blunt manner."

"Yeah, I guess I haven't changed much." There was a smile in his voice. "So you want to trek again? But..."

"I know I can do it." Okay, that was a little white lie. She knew no such thing. What she *did* know was that once upon a time, she'd been the fittest of the fit, and strong as hell. Her body had never failed her.

Until she'd failed it.

"Just try me," she said, hating the desperation she could hear in her voice. *Please just try me.* She needed this, needed to be outside, needed to feel strong enough for something.

"You always were a great guide," Keith admitted. "I guess, if you're serious, I have a camping trek next week in the Sierras. It's high-altitude though," he warned. "And high summer. It's also seven to ten miles of walking for four days running."

"I can do it," she said quickly, even as she paled at the thought of pushing her body that hard.

"Well, once upon a time no one knew that area better than you," he admitted. "Should be right up your alley. Pre-trip meeting is in three days, my offices."

She smiled, and that alone felt...amazing. She would do this, and she'd feel worthwhile again, alive. "I'll be there."

"I guess a trip like this will be good for you, huh?"

Good for her? Probably not.

But something to do, a direction to go in?

God, she hoped so.

OUTDOOR ADVENTURE'S offices were located in a large but old art deco building right on the bay. Twice she drove by looking for a parking spot. There wasn't one. There was never a parking spot in San Francisco, anywhere.

She glanced at the magazine on the seat next to her—the one with the Adrenaline-Rush article, which she'd bought for herself to keep staring at.

Risk.

Yeah. She was risking, all right.

Just then a parking spot opened up right in front of Keith's building. It was a sign, she thought, a sign that she was doing the right thing, and she put on her blinker and—

And nearly crashed into a brand-new Lexus, whose driver was going for the spot at the same time.

Her truck a mere inch from his, he looked at her through his designer sunglasses.

Oh, no you don't, she thought, and pointed to the spot and then to herself. *Mine.*

Lifting a brow, he cocked his head, as if not used to being told no.

Well, she had plenty of nos for him, but then he did something she didn't expect. He waved her into the spot.

Go ahead, he mouthed, his glasses slipping down his nose. Pushing them up, he again waved her forward. *Take it.*

Huh. Go figure. He wasn't a jerk. She watched as he put his car in Reverse, giving her room to take the spot.

Still dazed by this, she pulled in. By the time she got out of her car, he was gone, probably having to drive to Seattle to get his own spot.

That's when she looked up and saw it. The handicap

tag she'd been given after her injury, hanging off her rearview mirror. The tag she hadn't used in months but had never removed.

He'd given her the spot out of pity.

Well damn if she didn't hate that all the way down to her toes and back, where it settled into her gut like a slow burn. She didn't need the charity spot, damn it. Yanking the sign down, she stuffed it beneath her seat. Uncomfortably unsettled, she got out of her truck, refusing to admit to the shooting pain in her legs, the one she always got when she first stood up.

She ignored it. Her doctor had said she was healed enough to walk from here to the ends of the earth, which she'd taken to mean she could certainly lead others there, or anywhere else she chose.

Shooting pain or not.

The San Francisco night was cool for July. Summer still hadn't really kicked into gear yet, and as usual, probably wouldn't until it was nearly over. Didn't matter. She loved the misty air, the salty breeze, but it was time to get back to the mountains.

Yeah, if you can really actually do this...

Swallowing the doubts, she moved up the steps. Ahead of her was a man, tall and lanky, with short dark hair, dressed in clean, neat lines that would have looked just right on the pages of a glossy men's magazine. He held some sort of digital device in his hand, an earphone in his left ear, and was typing something at the speed of light with only his thumb as he walked and talked to himself.

No, wait. He wasn't talking. He was singing. Singing badly off-key to...she couldn't hear whatever it was he heard through his earpiece, but she caught his words. He was definitely screwing up a good U2 song.

He slid the Sidekick in his back pocket, the display still lit up, suggesting he had incoming messages and/or a phone call, all of which he ignored to squat and pat a stray dog on the steps of the building.

The dog, a mixture of black and white and grunge, rolled on its back and exposed its belly for more petting, its huge tongue lolling out of its head in ecstasy.

"Good boy," the man said, taking a seat on the step in his well-fitting beige pants which meant he clearly didn't do his own laundry. "You're a good boy, aren't you?"

In answer, the dog drooled happily, his legs straight up in the air.

As Lily came level with them, they both looked up, the man letting out an easy smile.

Her parking spot savior.

2

IN RESPONSE to Lily's surprise, the man's mouth went from smile to grin, the kind that was instantly contagious, though she didn't understand why. Because for her, a contagious smile came from a different sort of man entirely: a rebel, a guy who could and would transport her, make her wonder what was going to come next, give her a sense of…adventure.

This guy, in his pretty-boy clothes and pocket full of toys was cute enough, but her geek alert was beeping an alarm as loud as his Sidekick. "I didn't need that parking spot," she said.

"Okay." He looked at her from hazel eyes that were more whiskey-brown than sea-green.

"You should have kept it for yourself."

He seemed amused. "Not used to gift parking spots, huh?"

She wasn't used to gift anythings.

Leaning in, he arched his brow. "A hint? The correct response is 'thank you.'"

Damn it, he was right. She hated that. "Thank you," she said, moving through the door he opened for her. *"Twice."* She moved past him into the building's lobby, refusing to notice how good he smelled, or that she could feel him watching her limp.

"You okay?" he asked, right on cue.

Her shoulders stiffened. "I'm good." To prove it, she moved past the elevators, toward the door to the stairs. "I'm going to take these since you spared me the trouble of having to hike in from Timbuktu."

He laughed, a sound that seemed to come easily, and for some reason, she turned to look at him. Laugh lines fanned out from those interesting eyes, assuring her that he laughed often. "Glad I could save you the trouble," he said. "Think of how much gas you'd have used going to Timbuktu and back." His Sidekick beeped again, and he reached for it. "Excuse me. If I don't get that, it self-destructs."

"Sounds dangerous."

"Yeah, it's not pretty."

Probably he couldn't make a move without something beeping or requiring his attention, and she wondered how a guy like that ever went to bed with a woman. Did he bring all his toys and leave them on the nightstand when he stripped? Not that she cared, but it was an interesting image, him naked, holding his PDA, saying "excuse me, honey, hold that thought while I get a text message."

While he worked, she did as she usually did with things that made her uncomfortable, she walked away, letting herself into the stairwell to begin the climb. Halfway up, she thought she was going to die, and had to bend down at the knees and gasp for breath, which really pissed her off.

Damned body.

When she finally made it to the offices, she opened Outdoor Adventure's door and immediately took a deep breath. Ah, she remembered this place fondly. There were still maps, topos and photographs of places from all over the world on the walls. The maps were dotted with pins signifying where Keith and his guides had taken people. Once upon a time, she'd been the yellow pins, but someone else had taken that color. From all around her came a familiar sense of energy and excitement, and she was assaulted with memories.

The first time she'd set foot in here, she'd been awed and thrilled and...excited. During her interview, Keith had sat on his desk, right in front of her, larger than life, gorgeous and sexy. He'd agreed to teach her to guide that day, a promise he'd kept.

After she'd lost her virginity on that desk.

Now the reception area was filled with a group of people, drinking sodas and nibbling on munchies—the custom pre-trip meeting. She took in the faces, and then one in particular—Keith's, and just like that, she was no longer quickly approaching her thirtieth birthday without a plan, but was a nervous eighteen-year-old.

"Lily," he said, and crossed the room toward her. His sun-kissed-wheat hair was still long to his shoulders. His baby blues, always smiling, had a few more laugh lines, but as was typical of a man, they only added character. At five-ten, his body was still whipcord-lean and tough, ready for his next trip or climb or adventure or whatever.

One never knew with Keith.

It'd been part of his appeal. She waited for the on-slaught of more emotions, but interestingly enough, they didn't come, and that disappointed her even as she knew it was silly. What had she expected, to immediately be transported back to "herself"?

Maybe a little, she admitted, no matter how unrealistic that had been.

Keith put his hands on her arms and pulled her in, kissing one cheek, then the other, lingering with both far longer than social decorum called for.

Not that Keith had ever been concerned with social decorum. He'd always done what he wanted, when he wanted, never caring what anyone thought. That had been incredibly appealing to her back then, and she smiled now, leaning into him as if he could infuse her with his strength, his zest.

"You look amazing," he said for her ears only, handing her a drink from a nearby tray. "Now let me introduce you to your group. Everyone," he called out, stopping the light conversation and chatter in the room with just the one word, apparently clearly still carrying charisma around in spades. "This is Lily Peterson." He squeezed her shoulder, smiled down into her face. "I've put her bio in your packet, but here's your chance to meet her in person and ask her any questions you've stored up."

Everyone began chattering at once, and Keith laughed.

Not Lily. She didn't often get nervous. After all, she'd once been stuck on a mountain in a blizzard with no hopes of survival, and she'd gone down a class-six rapid and had her kayak break apart on the rocks all around her. Hell, she'd fallen off a cliff and broken her back, to be told she'd never walk again.

But this first meeting of people...*this* got to her. She took a quick sip of her drink and forced a smile. "Hello, everyone."

"Let's start with Rose McCall." Keith gestured to the woman closest to Lily. "Rose is a real estate agent from downtown, and is looking for something new and fun to do with herself. Hence the hike."

Rose waggled her fingers at Lily. Her nails were long and purple-tipped, encrusted with diamonds. "Looking forward to this, let me tell you." She wore designer jeans, low on her curvy hips and so tight Lily had no idea how the woman moved. Her black halter top was covered in sparkles that matched her five-inch heels. Her carefully applied makeup masked her age, but Lily would have guessed late thirties.

The Woman on the Prowl, Lily thought as she shook her hand. "Nice to meet you."

Rose smiled. "Likewise. I have a question. How do you feel about sandals?"

"On the trail?"

"Yes. My feet like to be cool. My toes need to breathe."

"Probably they're going to want to breathe before and after the trip," Lily said as diplomatically as she could. "Boots are definitely best."

"Agreed," Keith said, and with his hands on Lily's shoulders, turned her toward the next group member. "And this *here* is Roland Rocklin."

Roland was a twenty-something guy dressed in all in black from head to toe, black fatigues, black form-fitting T-shirt, black combat boots, and he was so gorgeous Lily actually blinked.

"Rock," Roland corrected, and held out his hand, a movement that set off all kinds of rippling muscles to go with his engaging smile.

"Wrestler?" Lily asked, thinking *The Hottie*. She'd never say her labels out loud, but she'd always had fun characterizing her groups. And she was already—shocking—having fun.

"Boxer," Rock told her with a quick grin. "My trainer bought me this trip for my birthday, said I was a pansy-ass—er, a wuss if I didn't make it to the end."

"Oh, you'll make it to the end," Lily assured him. No one was giving up on her watch, not even her, not if it killed her. "We all will."

"Good to hear." Rock's gaze slid over to Rose, who was retying her halter top. When the material slipped, she caught it just before exposing a nipple.

"Oops." She laughed gustily. "Sorry, don't mind me. But let me just say, I do like the idea of all of us getting to the…*grand finish*."

Rock's tongue fell out. Lily figured he was lucky he didn't start drooling.

Keith cleared his throat. "Moving on. Lily, meet Jack and Michelle Moore." He gestured to the young couple on the other side of Rose. They were both dressed to the nines, and built like they lived in a gym, not to mention California-perfect blond. "The trip is their one-year anniversary present from Michelle's father."

"Present…or torture rack," Michelle said as they both shook Lily's hand.

"No torture," Lily assured her.

"Yeah. Um, I was wondering." Michelle leaned in. "If there's any way you could just *pretend* we went on this trip. You know, if my father asked."

Lily blinked. "Pretend?"

"Don't listen to her," Jack said. "We're going." He looked at his wife. "You agreed to go so you don't lose your allowance. If it's that important to you, you go."

Michelle sighed. "Fine. But...could we arrange for a later start time so we don't have to get up quite so early?"

Lily shook her head. "I'm sorry, no. We have to leave at eight."

Michelle pursed her perfectly glossed lips. "Eight is ungodly."

"That may be, but we have a schedule. It's the start time."

"Huh." She considered that a moment. "Well, what happens if someone's...say, like, late?"

Lily glanced at Keith, who simply raised a brow. Passing the buck. Something he was good at, she remembered. He didn't like to be the bad guy. "If you're late," she said gently but firmly. "You'll probably get left."

Michelle looked intrigued by that, but Jack shook his head. "Michelle."

"Oh, fine. We'll be there."

Behind them, the office door opened, and in came...

"Ah," Keith said, with a welcoming smile. "The last member of the group, Jared Skye."

The man who gave up parking spots, stopped to pet stray dogs and opened doors for temperamental women now had a name.

He smiled at Lily, and the oddest thing…something happened low in her belly. It was a pit of knowledge—by the end of this trip, they would have a history, this man and herself. Somehow, in some way, she knew it.

She just didn't like it.

He slipped out his earpiece and shook hands with Keith, who turned to Lily and brought her close to his side. "Jared, meet Lily, your guide."

Jared looked startled for one moment before carefully masking it, probably wondering how someone with a handicap sticker could possibly be a hiking guide. That, or worse, he was thinking she was some sort of fraud, and Lily ground her back teeth and cursed herself all over again.

Keith handed Jared a drink. "A word of warning with this one, Jared." He said this with a warm, intimate smile for Lily. "Don't be late for the takeoff, or trust me, your beautiful guide here will leave you standing in the dust. I've been there myself."

"I'll be on time." Jared tipped his glass toward Lily in a toast, eyes warm, smile genuine. "To a good start and a great trip."

Again, she experienced an unsettling little sizzle, and she gave Jared Skye a second look as they all drank to his toast. Sure his eyes were compelling with that odd mix of chocolate and sea-green, and yes, he had that contagious smile which mixed self-deprecation and good humor, but those things weren't enough.

Right?

Keith was dividing a glance between Jared and

herself, as if he could feel the inexplicable electric current. "You two know each other?"

"Not exactly." Jared smiled into Lily's eyes. "But I'm guessing that this time *I'll* be thanking *you*."

"I haven't taken you anywhere yet," she said. "You might hate it."

"You think so?"

She scanned his lanky frame, and was surprised to find her gaze lingering. His face was clean-shaven, and while not exactly pale, certainly not tanned and rugged from any amount of time spent outdoors. His clean athletic shoes had clearly never seen a trail. His glasses were slipping again, and she'd bet herself he'd lose them on the first day unless he put a leash on them.

No, he didn't look like much of an outdoor guy. He looked more like an indoor, hunched-over-a-laptop guy, but before she could find a nice way to say so, something in one of his pockets beeped.

"More digital equipment?" she asked. "What a surprise."

With a wry smile, he reached for the offending unit, flicking it off with his thumb without even looking at it. "Sorry."

Keith shook his head. "You're going to want to leave all that stuff behind, man."

"Really?" Jared slipped the PDA back in his pocket. "Why's that?"

"It takes away from the outdoor experience."

Jared turned to Lily, his glasses providing just enough of a glare that she couldn't quite read his eyes, even though she had a feeling he had no such problem reading her.

And again, an inappropriate zing of…something surged through her. *Crazy.* She really did prefer a stronger, tougher, more seasoned man, someone who knew his way on a trail, who could climb a mountain, kayak a rapid, someone with a love of an adrenaline rush. Someone like…Keith.

And yet she didn't experience that little frisson of heat when Keith looked at her…

Huh.

Jared was still smiling easily. "So you don't think I look like the camping, hiking type."

"I'm not here to judge you, just to guide you."

"Come on, tell the truth."

"Okay, no. Sorry. You don't seem outdoorsy to me. But I still think you're going to have a lot fun."

Sipping his drink, he watched her from those intensely gripping hazel eyes. "One thing I've learned is that looks can be deceiving."

And in maybe the most surprising thing of all, yet another thrill went through her, because suddenly, strangely, she hoped so.

THAT NIGHT, Jared Skye lay in his bed staring at his ceiling, thinking about what he'd done. A confirmed city rat, he'd taken a week off work, a rarity, to go on a trip. Not just any trip, but a *camping* trip, with rocks and bugs and no running water.

Definitely not the norm for him. In fact, he'd never slept outdoors, not once in his thirty-two years.

But if life had taught him anything lately, it was to go with the flow, and try the path less traveled. To seize whatever the day brought, especially if the day brought a slightly irritating, self-protective, sexy-as-hell guide leader into it.

This year he'd been given a second chance, a hell of a second chance, when he hadn't died as he should have. As a result, he no longer waited for things to happen. He made them happen. And that meant when he saw something of interest, he did what it took to get it.

Lily Peterson interested him.

It wasn't just a gotta-have-you naked interest either, though that had definitely been there, too. But a gotta-know-you-deeper interest.

With a woman his polar opposite.

It might seem completely illogical, this attraction, not to mention out of character, but since he no longer depended on logic to get him through the day, he didn't care.

Nope, it was all about living to the fullest, logic not withstanding …

When he finally fell asleep, he dreamed—no surprise—of his trekking guide, with her vulnerable eyes, with the polite smile she wore to hide her thoughts, with her tough little body that he wanted arching and writhing beneath his…

No surprise then that he woke up hot and bothered, and he had to laugh at himself, even as he wished he could dive back into the dream…

Instead he got up. His first camping trip was going to be even more interesting than he'd thought.

LILY SAT straight up in bed, panting for breath and just a little bit sweaty.

She'd dreamed of being in a kayak, fighting another kayak for the best spot on the river. The best kayaker she knew was Keith, but it turned out not to be Keith out there with her, but a guy with impeccable dressing habits, and neat, short hair and designer glasses, a guy with a rather goofy, contagious grin and a rangy body that wasn't sure or coordinated.

Jared Skye, still disturbing her.

She got up, showered away the aches and pains and lingering stiffness she'd never had before her forty-foot fall, telling herself better to feel pain than to be six feet under, feeling nothing at all.

She dressed and went to physical therapy, where she was laid flat as always by Eric, who'd missed his calling and should instead have been working for the government torturing war prisoners for information. She showered again, dressed again, and then shopped and packed for the trip, telling herself the butterflies in her stomach were hunger pains, not nerves.

But the nerves were there, quietly eating her alive.

After going over the topo maps, marking everywhere on the trail she wanted to hit, with alternate plans for unforeseen events such as one of the hikers not being able to get as far as she'd planned—or God forbid, herself—she drove to Outdoor Adventures to coordinate for the supply and canoe drops along the loop they'd be walking.

But instead of an assistant she got Keith himself, with his mischievous smile and teasing voice that brought her back. When they were done, he hugged her good-bye, letting his hands linger and his body press against her for just a beat longer than necessary.

And because it was what she thought she wanted, she let him.

"Maybe we should get a drink tonight," he said against her hair. "And toast tomorrow's trip."

She wanted to want what he was offering, but suddenly she realized she'd spent her energy on second- and third-guessing herself and her ability to handle this trip, to lead an expedition into the wilderness...not to mention the doubts over her long-term goals, oh, and her ability to support herself.

Or to have a relationship...

She had nothing left.

"I'm leaving tonight," she said, a decision she knew Keith wouldn't question because most of the guides, and probably many of their guests, left the night before as well, staying at inns or hotels closer to the trailhead, three and a half hours away.

He looked disappointed, but let her go, and by late afternoon, she was making the drive from the bay area to the Sierras. Highway 80 was wide open, the July foliage and growth in full bloom on the hills. As soon as she hit the grade, she flicked off the air conditioner and opened the windows, inhaling deeply to get the scent of the mountains: sage and pine and everything else that felt so much more like home than any city.

She was doing the right thing. It felt like the right thing. Already, smiles were coming faster and easier than they had in too long. She took another deep breath and felt some of the terrible tension that had been with her begin to dissipate.

Feeling like the little engine that could, she kept repeating to herself *I can do this, I can do this...*

She arrived at the B&B just after dark, and got a surprise in the form of a tall, lean and lanky man sitting sprawled in a recliner in the reception area, sipping a drink.

Short, almost buzzed hair. Casual but elegant clothes. Easy I'm-comfortable-in-my-own-skin stance.

Jared Skye.

At the sight of her, he rose, tugging out his perpetual earpieces. Reaching into his pocket, he pulled out an iPod and thumbed a switch, slipping it back into his pocket.

So much for leaving the electronics at home.

"Hey," he said warmly, and the most peculiar thing happened.

She found herself smiling at him.

He smiled back, his eyes heating. "You staying here tonight, too?"

"Yes." Okay, this was bad. She'd wanted to be alone, the last time she would be for four days. "But..."

Looking into her face, Jared laughed softly. "Look at you, ever so thrilled to see me."

"I'm sorry," she managed to find enough grace to say. "It's...nothing personal."

For some reason, that had his grin spreading. "Oh yeah, it is. But that's okay." He flashed that smile again, the one that was slightly crooked, the one that made her feel inexplicably feminine, and for some reason, also made her want to take off her clothes.

"Why don't you join me," he said. "I'll get you a drink."

"Uh…"

"Come on," he said. "I promise not to ask you if I can wear open-toed sandals on the trip." He laughed at the look on her face. "Jack and Michelle told me. It's going to be an interesting trip, huh?"

"Very."

He steered her to the couch, and though he surely saw her limp, he didn't say a word.

But she had to. "About that handicap sticker," she said. "It's old. I don't use it."

He was quiet a moment while he sat. "As one who's had his own sticker, I get the whole love/hate thing over it."

She looked at him in surprise. He seemed perfectly healthy. His gaze met hers, dark, still warm but now filled with a whole host of memories, some painful, and in that moment, something happened. Something not physical, and not quite describable.

She didn't understand. He looked like a professor, sitting there with those glasses, the khaki trousers, the white button down shirt. A sexy professor, she'd give him that. He was studying her in that disconcerting way he had, seeing far more than she meant him to. "You're good now?"

"Yes."

She nodded. "Well, you're going to want to leave those pretty-boy clothes at home."

He looked down at himself, then arched a brow. "Pretty-boy clothes?"

She just arched a brow back.

His eyes lit with good humor. "Pretty-boy clothes. And here I thought I was so smooth. Go figure."

Damn, he made her want to laugh, too. "Well, they're fine, if you want to ruin your expensive things…"

"It's just money."

"Spoken by a man who's probably never had to do without."

"Ah, there you go again. Judging a book by its cover."

She opened her mouth, then slowly shut it. "You know, I think I'm going to bed before I put my foot in my mouth again."

"Wait," he said when she stood up.

"I'm sorry. I'm…not really fit for company."

His gaze ran down the length of her, then settled on her face. "You look plenty fit to me."

"Yeah." If he only knew. "I should—"

"One drink. If I annoy you before you finish it, you can leave." He slid a hand on her arm. "What do you say?"

His touch electrified, and she stared down at his fingers. "Um…" *Wow.*

"Now that's interesting," he murmured.

He was close enough that she could feel his body heat seep into her bones, and though he was touching her nowhere other than his hand on her arm, she felt surrounded by him.

Not to mention his scent—that intangible, male scent that was…yum.

What was happening here?

Slowly he lifted his other hand, settled it on her arm, too, and gently pulled her a little closer. His expression mirrored some of her own discomfort. "This isn't the light and fluffy sort of attraction I'd told myself it was."

"It's nothing."

A ghost of a smile curved his lips. "You don't feel it." He shook his head, laughed at himself. "Right. I should have figured that part."

Within sharing-air distance as they were, he was close enough that she could see gold specks dancing in those hazel eyes, filled with disappointment now.

Damn. She'd have thought she'd feel this attraction for Keith, had *meant* to feel this for Keith, but the truth was, she hadn't wanted to stare into Keith's eyes, and she sure as hell hadn't wanted to press her face to Keith's throat and inhale deeply. *Yeah, time to go.* "Good night," she said. "I'll see you at the trailhead. In jeans, I hope."

No smile tugged at his mouth this time. "'Night," he said, and dropped his hands from her.

With a nod, she turned away and headed for the stairs, and then realized something. She'd come here to find herself, to find some semblance of the person she'd been.

But that person she'd once been would have never shied from anything. At that thought, she stopped. "Jared."

"Yeah?"

"I…"

"You…"

"Feel it." She shook her head. "I just don't want to."

"Huh. Have to admit, I'm not sorry." His gaze lit with something that looked like both heat and laughter as he came toward her.

She stood her ground, her nose quivering because God, he smelled good, he smelled *heavenly,* and she was sniffing at him. "I really do have to go. I have to go to my room, I need to look over some maps and—" *And think about you...*

"I'm sure you've planned out this trip to the nth degree." He snagged her hand. "You deserve a night to relax before four days of work."

Relax? She'd been doing nothing *but* lying around healing for months, and if she hadn't managed to relax by now, it wasn't going to happen. In fact, if she stayed down here with him, with his hand downloading little electric currents of lust into hers, she knew she'd start sniffing him again, and then...who knew. "I really..." She trailed off when he waited patiently. "I really have to go."

"All work and no play." He laughed softly when she frowned. "I wouldn't have guessed that about you. Come on, Lily. What's your poison?"

"Excuse me?"

"What would you like to drink?"

"You don't have to serve me."

"How about, I want to?" He was close again, and she looked away because, oh boy, just looking at him smile was like looking at an unopened bag of barbecue potato chips—both irresistible and extremely bad for her.

Very bad.

"Wine?" he asked, looking at ease, looking confident, looking so freaking sexy it took her breath. "Beer? Soda? Painkiller?"

"Um, what?"

"The limp. You must be in some pain."

"Oh. That." The reminder slammed home all of her fears about this trip. "It's nothing. A beer, I'll take a beer." She took a step back, came up against the wall with a crash. "I'll take it to go."

"Lily—"

"No." She looked into his disconcertingly gorgeous eyes, and took a big step back—thankfully missing the wall this time—and an even bigger mental step. "Really. I'm sorry, I need to…" *Get my bearings.* "Go."

She accepted the beer he bought her, thanked him, and ran upstairs, where she put herself to bed.

Of course she dreamed of him again. That was getting extremely unsettling, she told herself at 3:00 a.m. after waking up sweaty, hot and bothered for the second night in a row. Why did her attraction to him bother her so much she wondered.

Because she'd expected it to be Keith?

Yeah, that. She punched her pillow, flopped over, and told herself to dream about something more worth her time—such as the fact she had four great days ahead of her.

Please God, let them be great.

She gave her pillow one more punch for emphasis, and then closed her eyes. Mountains, she told herself. Think of the mountains, the wild animals…

Only problem, her brain didn't obey, not one little bit. This time she dreamed about not taking her beer to go, but sitting downstairs with Jared, then making her way to his room, and then…

Oh boy, and then.

She should have taken Keith up on his offer for a drink with whatever else that might have entailed. It would have been easy, familiar, fast…and done.

Certainly if she had, she'd at least be sated by now.

And not still thinking, wondering, yearning about Jared.

3

JUST PAST DAWN, Lily stood at the trailhead at the basin of Balsam Peak and stared up at the vista of glory around her.

Doubt was killing her but she tried to swallow it. She could do this.

She could.

The summer hadn't been a particularly dry one, and as a result, the green mountains seemed to pulse with life. The Sierras didn't have a fancy name, or a photogenic centerpiece like other mountain ranges did, but man oh man, it was, in her opinion, one of the most fascinating combinations of jaw-dropping beauty and unique geology on this side of the Great Divide.

Being here, breathing in the thin but crisp, clean air, she felt great, and even greater when she realized she was way ahead of schedule.

That was old habit, being prepared beyond any shadow of a doubt. She credited that slight anal tendency in an otherwise carefree, wanderlust existence to the two years she'd spent as a Girl Scout as a young girl, when she'd been directionless and desperate to please. Her mother had worked around the clock, her father had been living in Europe somewhere, which had left her alone much of the time.

Too much of the time.

But she'd grown up fine. Or so she told herself. She was her own woman who didn't need approval from anyone. Knowing it, she opened the tailgate on her truck, and also the shell, and began checking through the supplies she'd brought, dividing it into piles that she could help her guests load into their packs as well as her own.

"Looks heavy."

Craning her neck, her gaze collided with Jared's. "Not too heavy."

He'd lost the business wear but was no less put together in his expensive-looking jeans and polo shirt. He wore hiking boots, which she sincerely hoped weren't new, even though they looked it. His designer sunglasses were firmly in place. "Need any help?" he asked.

"Not yet, thanks."

"How did I know you'd say that?" He gestured to the goods. "Looks like a lot of stuff to carry."

"If you're not up for it, you could always try a different type of vacation. Say a dude ranch."

Uninsulted, he let out a soft laugh, then shoved his sunglasses to the top of his head, revealing that mesmerizing hazel gaze as he slid his hands in his pocket. He pulled out a folded piece of paper, stared down at it, then slid it back into his pocket.

"What's that?" she asked.

"A list."

She waited for more, but he offered nothing. "A reminder to pick up your dry-cleaning?"

He smiled. "No."

"Ah. A reminder to have your housekeeper pick up your dry-cleaning."

His smile spread. "You think I'm going to be a PITA."

"PITA?"

"Pain in the ass. Your ass."

Not exactly. She thought he was going to be a distraction. A sexy one. "Caught me." She went back to separating the supplies into piles, but he didn't take the hint and leave.

"It bugs you," he said. "Our attraction."

"No, it doesn't."

He just smiled a little knowingly, and she let out a sound that she hoped managed to convey her annoyance as she went back to her work.

Okay, so despite his pretty-boy appearance, he wasn't prissy, or afraid of confrontation. Damn it. It didn't help that he was right.

Their attraction bugged the hell out of her.

Fine. She'd get her revenge soon enough, when she planned to see him plenty rumpled, wrinkled and pushed outside his comfort zone. "One thing's for sure," she said. "You're going to get those boots dirty."

He looked down. "I'm not going to melt with a little dirt."

"Okay."

He lifted his head, his eyes locked on hers. Normally she appreciated direct eye contact, but with him, the look went deeper than casual, and pushed her from *her* comfort zone.

"You don't believe me," he said.

She lifted a shoulder, and looked away because she had the uncomfortable feeling he saw far more than she allowed anyone to see. "It's your job to have a good time," she said. "It's my job to make sure you get that good time. I'll do my job."

"And I'll do mine," he promised. "I signed up for this trip willingly, Lily." He gestured with his chin toward the mountains. "I *want* to do this."

"Well, then let's get the show on the road. Oh, and though there's no rain or snow in the forecast—"

"Snow? In July?"

"It happens. Just make sure you packed everything on the list. Including raingear."

"Got it."

"And spray yourself with insect repellent. You got stuff with deet?"

"Yes, ma'am, just like the list said."

She ignored the gentle sarcasm. "It should be plenty dry, but the mosquitoes don't seem to care one way or another. They're vicious. Trust me, you'll get bites everywhere."

"Everywhere?" He asked this evenly but the humor was still swimming in his gaze, and also that unsettling heat.

Damn, he had quite the sense of humor. She loved a sense of humor. "Bites in certain places aren't funny," she said in the uppiest voice she could muster.

He stopped fighting his grin and let it fly.

Ah, man, he was something to look at, but she rolled her eyes and turned back to the truck. "Fine. But when you're walking bowlegged because your bites are chafing, I'll be getting the last laugh."

"I'll remember that," he promised.

"Good." She put her potion of the supplies into her pack, and it was a moment before she looked up again. When she did, Jared had moved back to his shiny, pretty car and was messing with something in his pack.

She let out a breath and told herself to concentrate on her fears and doubts. *That* should keep her nicely occupied.

But she took another peek. He was still fiddling with his stuff, and definitely not taking peeks at her. Good. Great. She went back to work, tossing the marshmallows into the pile. Which reminded her she needed to check the chocolate stash. If there was ever a trip that required extra loads of chocolate, this was it.

A truck with the Outdoor Adventures logo on the sides pulled into the dirt lot. The window went down. "Hey, gorgeous."

In shock, she stared, waiting for the burst of happy excitement. *"Keith?"*

He hopped out of the truck and spread his arms wide, looking tanned, fit and mischievous. "In the flesh."

"What are you doing here?"

He wore cargo shorts and a T-shirt with the logo on a pec, and he looked ready to guide. "You know I like to see a trip off."

She took in his rugged features, his slight smile, his heated eyes, and knew he wasn't here just for that. Once upon a time her sun had risen and set on him, a man ten years her senior and a hundred years older in so many other ways. He'd been the first strong male influence in her life, and for that alone, her heart warmed. "You were checking on me."

He shifted closer and put his hand on her shoulder as he peered past her to the food and supplies she was dividing up. "Just making sure you're okay. Should be a fairly easy trip." He gently squeezed. "You sure you're up for it?"

Why oh why wasn't she getting wobbly knees? Why weren't her nipples going happy? "I'm sure." *Liar, liar, pants on fire.*

"So tough, like old times."

She wished.

He touched her cheek and grinned, and she was reminded, vividly, of how, in the past, that grin would have melted her clothes right off. As if he was remembering the same thing, he shifted even closer. "Feels like old times." Nudging her body with his, he moved her around the side of his truck, where they were now out of view of anyone driving into the parking lot. They were also out of view of the only other car, Jared's Lexus.

Lily looked into Keith's smiling eyes, trying like hell to feel it, to feel the heat. "You're in my space."

"But it's such a nice space." They were toe to toe. He was only a few inches taller than her. It used to be she'd loved that, loved the way they'd lined up.

Everywhere…

Now his close proximity felt a little bit off, especially when compared to another man's recent close proximity—Jared's. She'd wanted to jump Jared's bones, which still made no sense. "Keith—"

"Hush a second." Cupping her face, he tilted it up and stared into her eyes. "I'm trying to see something."

"See what?"

"If it's still there."

"If what—"

"Shut up a sec, Lil." And he touched his mouth to hers.

She went very still. Not because she couldn't move away, but because she wanted to see, too. *Please turn me on...*

But no, nothing. Damn it. She cleared her mind and tried again, because surely it would come.

Keith slanted his head for better access, and touched his tongue to hers.

No fireworks.

No molten hot lava flowing through her veins instead of blood.

What was that about?

But deep down, she knew. It was about Jared, because *he* was the one she wanted. Oh, boy.

Keith lifted his head, staring sleepy-eyed down at her mouth. "*That's* how I should have greeted you yesterday." He stroked his thumb over her lip and smiled. "Have a safe journey, Lil."

And then he got back into his truck.

Blowing out a breath, she turned, and...

And her gaze locked with Jared's.

He'd moved around the front of her truck, raingear

in his hands. Clearly he'd come to show her he was prepared, and had caught more than she'd intended him to.

Now he stood there watching her with an inscrutable gaze.

Squirming, she shoved her topo maps into her pack. She had the route all marked, had everything planned, and yet suddenly, she felt...lost.

As a woman who'd always prided herself on knowing who and where she was, she hated the feeling. *When would she find herself, damn it?*

Jared turned away, and without another word, walked back to his car. She swallowed the urge to apologize. Damn it, she had nothing to apologize for.

Nothing at all.

WITHIN the next twenty minutes, the rest of the group arrived. Jack and Michelle came in a black Hummer driven by her daddy's chauffeur. When they got out and the car drove off, Michelle stared after it longingly.

"It's going to be fun," Jack assured her.

"I'd rather be having fun in Bali."

Jack sighed.

Rock showed up next, in a Jeep, and right after that Rose arrived in a taxi.

How she'd gotten a taxi up here, Lily had no idea, but Rose got out of the car, tossed the driver some cash, blew him air kisses, then straightened out her perfectly fitted, and possibly painted-on Daisy Duke shorts and barely-there camisole.

She did have on hiking boots, which she gleefully

showed off to Lily by lifting a leg and waggling her foot. "Cute, huh? I got a deal."

Her Daisy Dukes slid up an inch, to illegal heights really, revealing cheek, and quite possibly more to anyone off to the side of her.

Rock, in the exact right position off to the side of her, in the middle of an unfortunate sip of water, choked.

Rose smiled at him. "You okay, sugar?"

Rock choked some more, and Rose stroked a hand up and down his back, which didn't seem to help.

Eyes watering, gasping, he nodded that he was going to live and Rose stopped touching him.

Lily sighed. "Rose, you're going to want to change those shorts."

Rock, still hardly able to talk, shook his head. "Ah, don't do that."

Lily thought of the cliff they'd be walking along in less than an hour, and pictured the guys watching Rose's ass instead of the trail, then falling to their certain deaths. "Well..." How to be diplomatic here? "Those shorts aren't going to be comfortable."

"Honey, these are as comfortable as anything I've got."

Wasn't that just perfect?

Michelle came close. She slipped into a sunshine-bright yellow rain jacket that required sunglasses just to look at. "Which direction are we traveling in?" she asked anxiously.

"It's not going to rain, at least not today," Lily assured her. "You don't have to wear—"

"She's never camped before," Jack said. "She's nervous."

So that made two of them, Lily thought.

"Which direction?" Michelle asked again.

"It's going to change quite a bit out on the trail," Lily told her.

Michelle shook her head, her pretty blonde hair artfully layered about her face. "Can't you estimate? I want to leave a note here at the trailhead, so that if we get lost—"

"I can promise you that won't happen if you stick with me," Lily said. "I know this trail—"

"Which direction?" Michelle's voice came out high-pitched and just a little panicked.

Jared slid a palm-held unit out of his pocket and thumbed a few buttons. "North by northwest," he said, and showed Michelle the digital compass he'd pulled up. "See?"

Everyone leaned in to see the new toy, oohing and aahing, and Lily sighed again. "I thought the digital stuff was going to stay at home."

He looked right at her, for once his eyes not quite as warm—reminding her that he'd witnessed Keith's kiss—and without a word slid the unit back into his pocket.

Something went through Lily at that. Her own regret? Yeah, probably. But she had plenty of other stuff to worry about. "If everyone could bring their packs," she said. "I have the supplies divvied up for you to put away."

JACK LIFTED Michelle's pack for her, and shouldn't have been surprised to find it weighed more than his wife. "Damn, Shell. What did you put in here, rocks?"

She sent him a pout over her shoulder that he recognized well as he buckled her in. "It's way too heavy for me."

"Uh-huh," he agreed. "I told you that you packed too much."

"Don't start in on me. You want to please my daddy and his money as much as I do."

Ah, back to their biggest bone of contention, he thought with a sigh—which was that it wasn't just him and her in this marriage, but him, her and her daddy.

He loved Michelle, loved her more than he loved any other thing on this planet, but sometimes she drove him absolutely insane.

How could someone so smart be so incredibly dense? "I could care less about his money," he said patiently, for what had to be the bazillionth time in their one-year marriage.

"Right."

Jack shook his head. What made him think he could ever win this argument? He was coming to understand that what he'd heard was true—sometimes love just wasn't enough. "At least take out the ten pounds of makeup and hair products."

"I need it."

"You don't."

"My hair fuzzes at this altitude."

He shook his head. She was gorgeous, at any altitude. "So braid it."

"*Jack.*"

He groaned and tossed up his hands in defeat. "Might as well call back our driver, you'll be done by noon."

She looked horrified. "You know we can't back out. Daddy'll cut us off."

Right. And in her mind, that would be a fate worse than death. Heaven forbid they make this work like the rest of the world—on their own. God, she infuriated him.

But she also loved him as no one else ever had, and for that alone, he intended to give this all he had. "Look, just because your father is richer than sin, doesn't mean he can make us—"

"He's not making us. He just said that if we wanted to keep spending his money, we had to do this. He thinks we need the togetherness."

"He's making us," Jack said flatly, and turned his back on her to tend to his own pack, frustrated and…sad. Damn sad, because as much as he didn't want to believe it, he was afraid they—he—couldn't fix this enough to make it work.

LILY WAS HANDING OUT the supplies for everyone's packs when Michelle came up to her, still wearing her sunshine-yellow rain jacket. "Um…I don't have extra room."

Everyone had read the brochures. They'd been to the meeting, where they'd gone over the particulars of the trip in minute detail, including the fact they'd be helping carry the supplies. "Your portion isn't more than a few extra pounds—"

"But my pack's already too heavy."

"Damn right, it is," Jack said dryly, then lifted his hands when Michelle glared at him. "Hey, you needed your makeup and hair stuff, right?"

Michelle let out a huff and opened her pack. "Fine. Bye-bye hair products. But if I look like a Bohemian in a day, you all have no one but yourselves to blame."

"We'll keep that in mind," Jack told her and winked at Lily.

Michelle took the supplies from Lily. "This doesn't look like enough food for four days."

"We'll be getting two drops with additional supplies, so we don't have to carry it all right now. Just your own things."

"Right." Michelle looked at her pack. "That's going to be incredibly taxing."

Jack let out a huffing laugh. "For once, baby, we're in total agreement."

Yeah, Lily thought, she was going to have her hands full with this group. So far, she had a couple clearly on the outs, a woman on the prowl, and a man who was going to be said woman's lunch.

Jared, wearing his pack, moved into her line of vision, an enigmatic man of few words with a set of eyes that made her both yearn and want to run for the hills.

And a man *she* wanted for lunch.

"Lily, honey?" This from Rose. "I think you're right about the shorts. I'm going to change." She leaned in and whispered, "Wedgie City." Straightening, she held up two choices; a denim mini-skirt, or a pair of black Spandex short shorts. "Which would you suggest?"

Lily stared at them. "Uh...I really couldn't say—"

"No problem, I'll wear one today, and one tomorrow." Twirling away, she spared a moment to wink at Rock.

Rock, looking a little dazzled, shifted closer to Lily. "I could take on some extra weight for anyone who can't handle it—"

"That's very generous—"

"For a favor."

Lily looked at him. "Which is?"

"My tent goes next to hers." He nodded toward Rose and grinned, and Lily had to laugh.

"That's not my decision," she said. "It's between you and her."

"Hopefully, it'll be my prize for making it through the day."

She looked him over in surprise. So she wasn't the only one nearly paralyzed with doubt. "Why wouldn't you make it through the day? You're the fittest one here."

"Yes, but…" He grimaced, and spoke even more softly so no one could hear. "I'm indoor-fit, you know? Gym-rat fit. I've never spent much time outdoors, and I've certainly never spent four days straight walking through the woods."

"You put down on your application that you've camped."

Guilt flashed over his features. "Uh, yeah. I've camped. In my bathtub with G.I. Joe, when I was seven."

"Oh boy." Lily rubbed her forehead while Rock winced.

"Yeah, sorry about that," he said. "So maybe you'd better tell me now." He looked adorably nervous, this big hunk who'd camped with action figures. "Is this going to be too hard for me?"

"Are you kidding?" Lily gestured to Rose and Michelle. "I'm going to go out on a limb here and predict you're still way ahead of the game."

He flashed another grin. "Thanks."

Lily moved to the front of the group, ready to go, but before she could say so, Michelle sidled close once again. "I've got to talk to you," she said, sounding tearful. "I really don't think I can carry everything…"

"You could lose any of the five pairs of shoes you're toting," Jack suggested.

"But I brought one pair for each day, and then an extra. I'm not repeating, Jack."

"Tell you what," Lily said. "You lose the shoes, and I'll divide up your portion of the food and supplies between myself, Jack and Rock, who generously offered to help."

Rose looked at Rock, shooting him a sweet smile.

Rock blushed.

"Great," Jack muttered. "I get extra, and Rock gets lucky."

"Oh, come on, Jack," Michelle said. "Just help me here. After all, you like daddy's money as much as I do."

Jack shook his head. "There's no arguing with you."

They moved aside to fix her pack.

Jared shifted next to Lily, and she looked at him, already tired. "You have a request, favor or demand, too?" she asked in that voice she used sometimes, the one that said, Hurry because she was a little too busy for this.

But damn it, she didn't want to discuss anything, *especially* not the kiss between her and Keith, or the fact that she wished it had been with Jared.

She really wished that.

He just arched an eyebrow.

At that, she had to let out a careful breath and remind herself that he couldn't read her thoughts. "Is that a yes or no?"

He shook his head, looking quite comfortable in his own skin. "Nothing at the moment, thanks."

"Uh-huh. But you're reserving the right to make a later demand, is that it?"

His mouth curved, and he let their gazes stay locked for just a beat or so past what was comfortable.

Most definitely, he was thinking about the kiss.

And maybe, just maybe, he was thinking he'd rather it had been him, too.

He let her absorb that a moment, then turned away.

Lily let out another careful breath. Oh yeah, it was definitely going to be a hell of a trip.

4

As Lily checked and rechecked each person's pack and straps, Jared moved to the front, just next to the trailhead sign. With some amusement, he watched his group's fearless leader take control of the trip with clear-cut and concise directions and expectations for her guests, her fawn-colored hair pulled in a single braid that fell between her shoulder blades.

He loved how she looked, wearing cargo shorts low on the hips, fitted, but with enough pockets to outfit a third-world country, and two tank tops layered over each other, the top one with Outdoor Adventures' logo over a breast. She was the picture of efficiency and completely in charge.

She did like to be in charge, his Lily.

He understood the need. In his life, which until recently had been consumed with work, he'd always been in charge, as CEO of an international, billion-dollar corporation that created and built parts for all things digital.

Until that control had been taken from him.

"Any last questions?" Lily asked, coming up next to him.

"Yeah." He slid on his sunglasses and smiled. "Are you going to hurt me?"

She glanced at Michelle, flapping her lips at her husband, at Rock tying and retying his boots, at Rose applying lip gloss, and she sighed. "Somehow, I don't think you're going to be the one hurting."

This close, he could see that there was something in her eyes, that light of vulnerability he'd seen last night, and also…nerves. "But you are," he said. "Hurting."

She looked away. "I'm fine."

Yeah, she was pretty damn fine. But no matter what she said, she'd been hurt—the limp attested to that—and she wasn't all better yet. He felt a hard tug of empathy, because he knew what it was like to want to get better, to try to prove everything was normal when it wasn't. Yeah, he'd been there, done that and bought the T-shirt.

They began to walk, Lily in the lead. Her pack covered much of her from view. There was a light morning breeze which had loosened some silky strands from her braid. They flew about her head like a halo, which he imagined would piss her off but he liked it. He could see her ass, which was sweet, and her legs churning up the path ahead of him, although a bit unevenly, as if she had something to prove.

He thought maybe she did.

They all followed beneath a nicely warming morning sun touching down on the jagged peaks all around them, the rays gilding the treetops. Jared looked up and felt surrounded by them, a huge awe-inspiring circle of rocky, remote mountains he hoped to know a lot more about before he got back.

"This region is one of the most geologically young

and tectonically active in North America," Lily said, looking in charge of her world as she turned to face them, walking backwards.

Their eyes met and Jared felt the bolt he'd experienced the first time he'd seen her. Hell, every time he saw her. At first, it had been a purely physical sort of bolt, and there was still plenty of that, but somehow also more.

Much more.

Which suited him just fine. It'd been a very long time since he'd felt such a punch of attraction. Granted, he'd had other things on his mind—like surviving...

But he was past that now, and living life to its fullest, going after everything he wanted.

He wanted her.

Or he had before she'd kissed her boss...

"Are there volcanoes?" Michelle asked Lily, sounding nervous.

"Not here," Lily assured her. "Though this mountain system does straddle several of the earth's moving plates, huge forces that continuously build this sweeping arc of mountains—see how rugged and craggy the peaks are? It means they're still very young, comparatively. Just babies, really."

"Pretty big babies," Jack said beneath his breath, making his wife laugh breathlessly in agreement.

"Were there dinosaurs here?" Rose asked.

"Oh, yes," Lily said. "Back in the day."

"The Mesozoic Era," Jared offered, then smiled when Lily looked at him, clearly startled at his knowledge.

"I'm impressed," she said. "What else do you know about this area?"

"Other than there are big bears and that I shouldn't feed them? Not much."

Michelle scooted closer to Jack, a bright yellow spot of sunshine in her raingear. "Bears?"

"Don't worry," Lily said. "No one's going to be bear bait on this trip."

"So how high are these babies anyway?" Jack asked, pointing to the highest peak ahead.

"Nearly fifteen thousand feet at the top."

"That's like, three miles high," Rock said, with a low whistle. "Man, we're going to be huffing and puffing."

They were already huffing and puffing. Jared sure as hell was. But the exercise felt good. Actually, it felt amazing, especially after so many months of being able to do so little. The air held a silence that he never heard in the city, and that felt good, too. Not having to think, work…

Gradually, the distance between the group members widened as they moved up the trail that took them to breathtaking heights, along stark ridges and drop-away cliffs.

He kept up with Lily with surprising effort. "You're looking pleased with yourself," she said, breaking a long silence.

"I am pleased," he said. "To be here."

She smiled, a real one, he realized with some pleasure, and it lit up her entire face. "I know. Me, too. I'd— You know what? Never mind."

"No, what?"

"I'd worried that I wouldn't be able to hold up," she admitted.

He nodded, knowing that was quite a confession for her. "You and me both."

She smiled at him, and it was a beautiful thing.

"It's such a perfect day for this," she said. "Not too hot, not too cold."

"I'm definitely just right."

She looked him over, and bit her lip.

"Go ahead," he said on a laugh. "Mention the clothes."

"Okay, so you had the right clothes after all."

She was genuinely amused, and he liked the look on her, very much. She was naturally fair-skinned, which meant she had an adorable smattering of light freckles over her high cheekbones and nose, though he doubted she'd appreciate the word *adorable*. Her eyes, so light brown they looked like crystal-clear amber, or a very expensive whiskey, sparkled. "Are the jeans brand spanking new?" she asked.

"I'll have you know, I've owned these for years."

She fingered his crisp T-shirt, worn beneath an open long-sleeved blue chambray shirt. "You ironed this."

"No." But probably his housekeeper had. "Maybe."

She laughed and eyed his hiking boots. "Those aren't—"

"Not new. They're broken in, I promise." He grinned at her inspection. "Let's hear it. Any complaints?"

She took her gaze on a tour along his body. Did those eyes heat as she brought them back up to his, or was that his hopeful imagination?

"No complaints," she finally said, sounding just a little breathless now.

Not his imagination...

The words dissipated any last chill from the morning air, that was for damn sure. He might have been sick this last year, very sick, but apparently certain things, like a healthy lust, never left a man.

Thank God.

That's when the digital ring of a cell phone pierced the air.

His.

"Oh, no, you didn't," she said.

"Sorry." He pulled the cell out of his pocket, eyed the ID, then sighed as he flipped the phone open. "Hey, Candace."

"Hey right back atcha," his fearless and irreplaceable assistant said cheerfully. "Just calling to say it's not too late to come to your senses. I could have a helicopter there to get you in half an hour."

"I'm doing this."

She sighed. "Thought you'd say that. All righty then, have a safe trip. Oh, and don't get bitten by a rattle-snake. We did not nearly lose you this year to watch you go down so easily."

"I'll stay away from snakes, I promise."

Lily's pretty eyes were narrowed when he shut the phone. "How did you get service up here?"

"Satellite."

"No cell phones on this trek."

"Is that a hard and fast rule?"

"It's just that you're paying me a lot of money to take you away from all that. If you'd wanted to talk to the girlfriend, you should have just brought her with."

"Assistant, not girlfriend."

"Oh."

Was that just a smidgen of relief on her face, he wondered, or his own healthy imagination? "Don't worry, Lily. I'm ready to be taken away."

She looked at him for a long moment, then back at the others, who'd slowed to their own various paces. He knew she was going to move away from him and go check on each of them in turn, that he was nothing special to her, but he wanted to be. "I'm curious. Why do you guide?"

"Uh…" she looked back at him, distracted. "Because they pay me?"

"I doubt it pays that well, which means you must really love it." He looked around at the towering trees, the mountains, the sky. "I admit, it's beautiful, but you probably end up dealing with a lot of spoiled people."

"Yes, but I get paid to wander the wilds all day long…trust me, the pros outweigh the cons."

"I bet. Especially for a person with wanderlust."

She glanced at him, a long stray strand of hair across one eye. "Judging the book by its cover?"

His finger itched to touch that silky strand, to stroke it back behind her ear. Instead he laughed. "Are you going to deny you've got wanderlust?"

She looked away. And then, after a moment, sighed. "You have a way of seeing things I don't want you to see."

"Thank you."

"That wasn't a compliment." That said, she gestured him ahead of her, then slowed to talk to the others.

Rock stopped her, pointing to his boots. Lily slipped

out of her pack to bend down and take a look, saying something that made Rock relax a bit and even smile.

Above them, the sun continued to warm.

Lily straightened with a hand on her back and a wince on her face, which made Jared take a good long second look at her. She was hurting more than she'd let on. Hadn't he seen her do her best to hide a limp that couldn't be hidden? The woman clearly had pride in spades.

He knew all about pride. After the cancer there'd been people who looked at him differently, with pity and constant worry, treating him with kid gloves, and he hated that, so yeah, whatever her issue, he understood, and when she glanced at him, he looked away to give her a moment.

It wasn't a hardship to take in the scenery. Despite having lived in San Francisco all his life, he'd actually never been in the Sierras before. Funny, considering he'd been to Europe, South America, even Australia... But those trips had been all business and little else.

Up until recently, his entire life had been about business and little else. A classic workaholic, he'd worked around the clock, running his world with easy precision.

Now for the first time, he was allowing someone else to run his world, at least for the next four days. He glanced back at Lily, still messing with Rock's boots. If he could have drawn his fantasy woman, she'd have been it. Five-sevenish, she was fit and tight and toned. He doubted if she had an extra inch of flesh on her. And yet something about her was soft, warm...with that dash of vulnerability amongst the secrets she held.

As he watched, she hoisted her pack back up, which he knew damn well weighed a great deal more than any of theirs. Another wince as she set the thing on her shoulders, adjusted it, clicking the straps in just above her breasts and around her waist.

Jack and Michelle approached her about something. Lily reacted with some doubt, then went around to behind Michelle, adjusting her pack for her, while Jack just shook his head.

Rose had stopped to rub some suntan lotion on her legs, bending over in that short-short skirt, which had even his eyes crossing.

Rock's eyes didn't just cross, they about popped out, and he turned his head, glancing up at Jared with a sort of helplessly caught expression.

Lily walked past them all, moving back to the lead. "Rose, if any of the guys walk off this trail and fall, you're going to conduct their rescues."

"Oooh," she responded with glee. "Do I look that good? Really?"

"Yes," Rock said reverently.

Jack nodded.

Michelle smacked him. Then she looked at Lily. "How far are we going today again?"

"Seven and a half miles," Lily said.

"That sounds far. How much of that have we already done?"

"Uh…maybe a half mile."

"Maybe?"

Jared pulled out his PDA, thumbed a few controls, then looked up. "Point seven."

Lily gave him a long look, and with a smile, he slipped the PDA away.

She sighed, then turned back to Michelle. "Look. See way out there…" She pointed across to a neighboring peak, a long rock formation jutting out of the hillside. "We're going to camp there. It's got a grass floor. Very soft, very comfy."

Michelle looked intrigued. "Really?"

Lily smiled, though it looked a little bit like an athlete on a losing team trying to be a cheerleader. "And wait until mile two, you'll see huge trout in the river below. Dinner is going to be amazing."

Michelle swallowed hard. "Trout."

Jack leaned in. "Vegetarian alert."

Lily's cheerleader smile didn't slip. "Right. So you'll skip the trout. I have lots of food, never worry. Soon we'll be walking beneath hundred-year-old lodgepole pines, through big-buck country. Trust me, you'll love it."

"Okay." Michelle zipped up her raingear. "I'll trust you."

They all kept moving, up, up, up. Now they were several hundred feet off the meadow floor, with the river winding far below.

As the sun rose, the heat made little pillars of steam rise off the rocks, vanishing into thin air. They passed several impressive waterfalls that thundered and crashed to the valley floor. It was all both alien, and gorgeous. Jared inhaled deeply, the air feeling sharp and pure against his lungs. He'd never imagined himself doing this. As a confirmed city rat, he'd never given it much thought.

But, as he'd learned recently, life was about changes. Thankfully, he thought, this was a good one.

And still they walked…

It actually took him a while to settle into doing nothing with his brain, but once he did, his mind finally slowed. Relaxed.

Enjoyed.

He drew in another breath, and the scent of pine and sage and clean, fresh air filled his lungs again, without a hint of smog or gasoline, without the noise of traffic on busy city streets, without pain.

He really liked that part.

But the part he liked the best...was being right behind Lily. She practically quivered with determination, which he now knew to be a facade for her own nerves.

The woman was a walking marvel.

Even with her pack on, even with the limp, he enjoyed watching her body move. She had a way about her—utterly economical movements, no time wasted, nothing unnecessary, and yet she was so innately feminine, he just wanted to nibble on her.

But more than that, he wanted to hear her story. He had a feeling it would only strengthen her attraction for him.

The trail began to come down a bit in altitude, and he welcomed the easier going. They all settled into the cadence of Lily's stride. "Look," she said, and stopped, pointing to prints on the ground. "This one's a deer, and there are the wolves, trailing it."

Michelle gasped. "Oh my God. Did the wolf eat Bambi?"

Jack rolled his lips inward and looked at Lily.

Lily looked at Michelle for a long moment. "No," she finally said, and Michelle beamed.

They cut through a field of mossy grass high as their

waist, filled with wildflowers, the splashes of color so bright the scene looked like a painting.

Jared couldn't believe he'd gone so many years without doing anything like this. After so many years of nothing but work, and then nothing but waiting for fate to decide whether to give him a second chance, just walking all day felt…wonderful.

The day was glorious, not a single cloud in the brilliant azure sky. The jagged, starkly beautiful peaks jutted high and proud, some still white-tipped, as unbelievable as that seemed.

Birds chirped. Squirrels chattered. Beneath their feet the fallen pine needles crunched. From somewhere out in the woods surrounding them came a howl, which Jared could admit, gave him a moment's pause.

And still they walked.

"I get the feeling I should have taken my wife on a cruise instead of a hike."

Jared looked over at Jack, who'd caught up with him. "It said 'strenuous walking involved' on the brochures," Jared pointed out.

Jack sighed. "Yeah. Michelle didn't get the brochure."

"Well, then, I'd sleep with one eye open tonight if I were you."

Jack laughed, but the sound was mirthless. "I didn't pick this trip. See, Michelle's father…he's trying to save our marriage."

Strange way to do it. "Can it be saved?"

Jack glanced back over his shoulder at Michelle, who was muttering to herself about her shoes, about the altitude, looking very unhappy. She'd removed her yellow rainjacket, and tied it around her waist. "She's a mess," Jack said. "A sexy, gorgeous mess. Life would certainly be easier without her."

"You might be finding that out sooner rather than later, especially if she gives up."

"If we don't complete this trip, together, then her father is cutting her off. Allowance, trust fund, credit cards, all of it, bye-bye."

"Harsh."

"It's his money." Jack gave another shrug. "I couldn't give a shit about it. But she gives a shit. A big one."

"So you're doing this for her?"

"I guess I am."

"Maybe you care more than you think you do."

"Yeah." Jack sighed and glanced back at Michelle again, his expression softening as he did. "You know, call me an idiot, but just looking at her makes me ache."

Jared had been in relationships, but none had lasted. Candace moaned and groaned it was because he'd always worked too much, but honestly? He simply hadn't met the woman, The One, or at least nothing close to the love he'd witnessed between his parents for thirty years. They were a tough act to follow, and his relationships, while lovely and fun and exciting, hadn't been magical, or ever made him ache. He'd begun to figure it might never happen for him, but that had been before the Big Change.

Or so he called his near miss with the Grim Reaper.

Now he looked ahead, his gaze snagged on Lily's trim, purposeful figure as she led them along, her hips swinging as she went.

Now...he was determined not to miss out on

anything, especially a chance to find the woman to make him ache. But truthfully?

He had a feeling he might have already found her.

LILY KEPT turning back to face them, talking about the types of trees and plants and wildlife in view. He caught little of what she said, what with his gaze snagged on her sweet ass. As if she sensed it, she craned her neck, and caught him in the act. She did an almost comical double take, as if not quite sure that she'd seen what she thought she had.

He smiled, effectively but silently admitting that yeah, he'd been looking at her.

A breeze blew that stubborn strand of hair across her eyes, and she impatiently shoved it free, then with another long, adorably befuddled glance, turned forward again. Then her fair coloring gave her away when the skin on her neck pinkened.

He was in midgroan over that when from behind him, Michelle screeched.

JACK RAN TO HIS WIFE. By the time he got to her, Michelle was dancing around in circles, waving her hands. At her scream, his heart had jumped in his throat, but she looked okay to him. "Michelle? What's the matter?"

"Did you see it?" she cried, practically crawling up his body. He liked that part. A lot.

"It just ran across my feet. A rat, a huge rat!"

"Not a rat," Lily said, coming up to them.

Michelle pulled her face from where she'd plastered it against Jack's throat. "Well it wasn't a squirrel!"

"Probably just a marmot."

"Oh, my God! A marmot?" She looked at Jack, panicked. "A marmot!" She turned back to Lily. "What's a marmot?"

"They're harmless. He's probably scurrying around, snacking on leaves and bark."

"He was *fat.*"

"And happy with it, I'm sure. Don't worry, he doesn't eat much."

Jack laughed, and Michelle shoved free of him. "It's so not funny."

"A little bit it is."

They all started walking again.

"Jack," Michelle said after a few minutes. "Are you tired?"

"No."

"Oh."

Jack sighed. "Remember when you said I was getting a spare tire around my middle?"

Michelle swiped at her forehead, panting for breath. "I was just kidding."

"You were?" Perplexed, he glanced at her. Would he never understand her? "I didn't know that. I started running."

She blinked. "Is that where you go before the crack of dawn? Running?"

"I always tell you where I'm going." Always. He'd made sure of it. "Where did you think I was?"

Michelle gnawed on her lower lip.

"Michelle."

She rolled her eyes and turned away.

Oh, no she didn't. He grabbed her hand, tugging her around, shocked. "You thought I was cheating on you. Jesus. That's flattering."

"With Theresa."

"The maid? She's like eighteen!"

Michelle jerked a shoulder and swiped her forehead again.

Jack couldn't believe it. "I would never…"

"Okay."

He watched her trying to catch her breath. "Look, why don't I lighten your pack a little?"

"I'm fine."

"I thought your Pilates classes were helping you."

"I, um, haven't really been taking Pilates classes."

Jack's heart stopped again. "So what have you been doing? Or is this one of those things I don't want to hear until we're in divorce court?"

"Shopping," she admitted. "I haven't been cheating on you either. I've been shopping."

"Shopping." He chewed on that a moment. "But we're on a tight budget. Which means…" Ah, hell. "You've been using daddy's money again, when we agreed we wouldn't."

"Isn't that better than what you thought I might be doing?"

Jack sighed, and gave up. But why the hell was he so filled with tension and resentment if neither of them had been cheating?

THE DAY WARMED. As they continued along, insects began to buzz. The dew dried and fallen pine needles crunched more loudly beneath their feet. Lily was hurting, but no more than she'd be at home, after physical therapy.

She had no idea how she'd feel tomorrow, which did not loosen her knot of nerves.

Looking back, she watched as Rose picked a wildflower, and tucked it behind her ear, smiling at Rock.

Rock smiled back, and then she picked him a wildflower, too, making him blush.

Lily glanced at Jared, just a quick look, and he caught her. Damn it.

But she couldn't help but wonder if he'd like to tuck a wildflower behind her ear and claim her as his. Or if he'd rather take the flower and run it over her body, and then follow that path with his mouth…

She had no idea where these thoughts were coming from. No idea at all.

Okay, she knew. But that didn't mean she had to give in. "Almost time for lunch," she announced.

"Don't suppose we can radio for take-out," Rose joked. "Maybe some Thai?"

"Don't worry," Lily promised with a laugh. "I've got a lovely, luxurious lunch planned. No one is going to be hungry."

Jared's gaze met hers, and held.

She knew just how hungry he was, and exactly what he was hungry for.

Oh, boy.

5

AFTER LUNCH, they took up the hike again. Jared eyed the view as they came out of a rocky canyon, a sheer rock on their left, a drop-off on their right, the river winding below.

"I'd swear we've gone two hundred miles," Rose puffed. "Jared?"

He pulled out his PDA, glanced at Lily, who rolled her eyes. Damn, she was cute. "Four point six," he said.

"Or that," Rose muttered.

Once again they heard water falling, a different waterfall this time. "Almost there," Lily promised them, and then they cleared past the trees and paused at the heart-stopping, magnificent view.

The water fell down thirty feet or so, splashing with loud, wet grandeur into a large natural pool. The pool was surrounded by rocks, over which the water spilled, creating a second, smaller fall dropping into the river they'd walked along to get up here.

"Can we swim?" Jack asked.

"Not here. It's much safer from below, which we'll get to in the morning. Keep drinking everyone, no dehydration today."

"Okay, I get it now," Michelle said on a huffing laugh. "*This* is why Daddy wanted us to come on this trip. He wanted to kill us to save him the attorney fees for our divorce."

"We haven't decided to divorce yet," Jack said, then hesitated. "Not that I know of, anyway."

Michelle lifted a shoulder. "You've been so upset with me, I figured it's only a matter of time."

Jack's face went carefully blank. "Don't put words in my mouth."

"Fine, but switch places with me," Michelle said. "*You* walk in front so you won't be tempted to push me off the falls into the river."

"You know," Jack said thoughtfully. "That idea hadn't occurred to me."

"Oh," Michelle said.

"—until now."

"*Oh.*"

Rose smiled over at Rock. "Maybe you want to switch places too, sugar, and give me a better view."

Rock passed her. "Is that better?"

Rose eyed his ass. "*Waaay* better."

Jared watch Rock finally get it, and blush beet red. The trail was flat now, and he easily managed to stay right behind Lily. He figured he had the best view of all, and he enjoyed it until a squirrel popped out of a tree and screeched at him for getting too close, nearly giving him a coronary.

Lily looked back and smiled. "You're being scolded."

"Too close to his home?"

"Bingo."

Jared looked at the tree the squirrel had vanished into. "He's got a nice home."

"Gorgeous here, isn't it?" She took it all in and smiled with pleasure. "I almost forget, until I come back here."

"From…?"

"Oh. Well, I have an apartment in San Francisco, though until recently I spent most of my time as a wildland firefighter in Montana."

Yeah, he could see her as a firefighter, all sharp and toned and tough. "Sounds exciting."

"Was," she said, and rubbed her thighs.

It was a motion he'd seen her do before, and he doubted it was a nervous gesture. The trail widened enough that he could move to her side. "Something happen?"

"You could say so. A cliff happened."

"You fell?"

"Forty feet."

He stared at her, horrified.

"Yeah, that's the usual reaction," she said. "But at least I lived to tell the tale, right?"

"Right. Wow."

"Living was definitely the silver lining," she agreed grimly, then quickened her step as if she'd told him far more than she'd meant to.

"How bad was it, Lily?"

She lifted a shoulder. "Broke my back. They said I'd never walk." She shrugged again. "Proved them wrong."

He stared at her back as she kept walking, awed at her strength, and also, a little awed at the similarities in the things they'd suffered. "But you're recovered. That's amazing."

"Not so recovered. I can't be a firefighter anymore."

"It's amazing that you're out here at all, doing this." He shook his head. "You must have gone through hell to get here."

A mirthless laugh escaped her.

He looked at her proud, stiff shoulders, and imagined all that she wasn't saying. And if anyone understood that, it was him. "I'm sorry you had to give up firefighting."

"It was time for something new anyway."

One tough cookie. "Was it?"

"Yeah. I don't tend to stick to anything for long."

"You look happy doing this."

She paused, considered, then smiled. "You know what? I am."

"And Keith," he said carefully, well aware that he was now on a fishing expedition. "He must be thrilled to have you working for him."

"Oh." She glanced away. "We go way back, Keith and me."

He kept breathing, barely.

"But...this is my first trek for him in years, so we'll see how it works out."

He nodded. "He seemed happy enough with you."

She glanced at him, probably remembering the kiss he'd witnessed.

The hell with subtlety, he decided. "Are you two together?"

She took a long drink from her water bottle, a nice delay tactic, he noted. "I'm not sure that matters," she said carefully.

Reaching out, he put a hand on her arm and stopped her progress, pulling her around to face him. The others were all still far enough back that no one was in danger of overhearing. "You can't see why it would matter to me?"

"You're a client," she whispered.

"For a few days, that's all."

She licked her lips. Now that was *definitely* a nervous gesture, but he liked it. He liked her.

Much more than he'd intended to, when it'd once been a purely physical thing.

"We need to keep moving," she said, her gaze dropping for the briefest beat to his mouth.

Yeah, he liked that, too, but then she pulled free and began walking again.

She'd picked up her pace, and he had to hurry to catch up with her, which stole his breath and kept him, temporarily, from asking anything more.

"Your bio says you're some sort of electronics wizard," she said, because apparently *she* still had breath. "After seeing some of your toys so far, I believe it. How many did you bring, anyway?"

"Uh…"

She slowed down and let out a disbelieving laugh as he passed her. "You know what? Don't tell me."

"Okay." Turning to face her, he walked backwards, smiling as he thought of the iPod and the PDA he carried. Not to mention his Sidekick… "I won't."

"Hey, watch out—"

He turned forward just as she pushed past him to shove a large branch out of the way. If she hadn't, he'd have walked right into it, head first.

Feeling just a little bit stupid and a lot awkward, neither new when it came to beautiful women, he shot her a sheepish smile, which faded.

She'd gotten scratched across her neck.

"Ah, hell." He reached for her. "That was my fault. I'm so sorry."

She put a hand to her neck, then looked at her fingers, which had a little smear of her blood. "It's nothing."

He put his hands on her arms to stop her forward movement, and studied the scratch. True, it wasn't bad, but it bothered him just the same. He shrugged off his pack and squatted down to go through it.

The folded piece of paper fell out of his pocket again.

She looked at it. "I know. Your grocery list."

"It's a list, but not groceries."

"A to-do list."

"Sort of." He called it his To-Do-If-He-Didn't-Die list.

"What does a guy like you put on a list?"

A guy like him? What the hell, he handed it to her, then reached into the front zippered pocket of his pack for a tube of antiseptic and a Band-Aid.

She laughed at the first aid stuff. "You're kidding."

"See? And you thought I'd be totally unprepared. I'll have you know I also have sunscreen, waterproof matches, moleskin and aspirin."

"Nice." She peered into the pouch. "And a snake-bite kit?"

"Yep. And also water purification tablets."

"And the kitchen sink?" She unfolded his list and began to read.

He watched her face, and when she was finished, she handed the paper back to him.

"What do you think?" he asked, unable to help himself.

"I think that maybe everyone should have a list."

He'd never thought so until he'd made his. He had it memorized. One, take a guided trek in the mountains. Two, sail the Greek Islands. Three, eat less fast food and more seafood, even if it's slimy. Four, remember to smell the flowers. Five, tell the people in your life that you love them.

What would be on yours?" he asked her.

"You know, I have no idea." She lifted a hand. "All my life, if I've wanted to go somewhere, or see something, I've just done it."

"That's an amazing way to live," he agreed. "But there's got to be something you'd like to do that you haven't."

A shadow crossed her face, and she grabbed the antiseptic.

"Here. Let me." He took it back and stroked some of the cream over her skin, which felt like warm silk beneath his fingers.

Warm silk. He was thinking of warm silk. To take his mind off that, he reached for the Band-Aid, but she pulled away.

"It's just a scratch." Her body language said back off because she could take care of herself. Her eyes said he'd gotten too close, and not just proximity-wise.

What had spooked her, he wondered. The list? No, she didn't understand the significance of the list. Maybe it'd been the way he'd tried to take care of her scratch.

Had no one ever fussed over her before? And why did that make him want to do just that? "Does it sting?"

"No," she said, a bold lie that made him laugh softly. "Here." Putting his hands on her shoulders, he looked into her eyes as he tilted his head and leaned in. She inhaled sharply as he blew very gently across her neck.

"Jared—"

"Shh." He waited to see if she would, and when she clamped her lips shut, he took that as approval and did it again, blowing yet another breath over her flesh, which he noticed was now covered in goose bumps.

She shivered, and he knew damn well it wasn't from pain. "Better?" he murmured.

"Um—"

He lifted his head. "Because I have one more trick up my sleeve," he said, and kissed her neck, right above the cut.

She slapped a hand on his chest. "What are you doing?"

"Kissing it all better." He lifted his head and smiled into her shocked face. "Did it work?"

"I…" Looking adorably perplexed, she put her hand to her neck. Her voice came low and throaty. Incredibly sexy. "You kissed me."

"No."

"No?"

"Nah. Now this…*this* a kiss." Sliding his hand around to the back of her neck, he pulled her in, then stopped with his lips a mere whisper from hers. He absorbed the way her breath caught, the way his own did the same, including his heart.

Then he closed the distance…soft, wet, warm lips connected, her body an arousing heat against his.

She hadn't budged, not even to breathe since that initial little panting sigh, but he could feel her heart stammering against his, and then…then she took the hand on his chest and fisted it in his shirt, right above his heart.

He liked that, liked that so much he pulled her closer, and—

And from down the steep trail, Michelle called out. *"Lily?"*

With a sigh, he made himself ease back.

Lily didn't take her eyes off Jared's. "Here! We're up here!"

The others straggled along while Lily continued to stare at Jared.

He smiled.

She touched her neck again, as if not sure any of it had really happened; the scratch, the kiss… "Just about there," she called out, and with one last look at Jared, she turned and kept walking.

With the taste of her still on his lips, he followed, the walking helping to clear his muddied-up heart. As far as the eye could see lay peaks and valleys and wide alpine meadows like green inland oceans, blanketed by a sky of sheer azure blue. The falls crashed loudly ahead, dropping into one of those green seas.

They were at the top of the world.

"Here," Lily firmly said, and dropped her pack.

Everyone dropped their packs, too. Rose swiped her brow and smiled as Rock handed her a canteen of water. "What a sweetie, thanks. A big built cutie like you, you must spend a lot of time doing stuff like this, huh?"

"No," he said, swiping his brow with his arm. "This is my first time."

"Ah," Rose said speculatively. "A virgin."

Rock went beet red. "No, I—"

"An outdoor virgin." Rose smiled. "Goodie. We can lose our cherries together."

Rock couldn't say anything, having probably swallowed his own tongue.

Rose look around. "Bathroom?"

"Bushes," Lily said.

"Oh my." She looked at Rock. "Will you stand guard?"

"Sure."

"Jack? Michelle?" Lily asked as they sank to the ground and leaned back against their packs. "Okay?"

"Great," Jack said, actually looking like he was enjoying himself.

"Great?" Michelle asked him incredulously. "You're doing great?"

"Well...yeah. You?"

"My pack's too heavy and my feet hurt."

"You knew this was going to be hard. I thought we were going to make the most of it."

She piled her long, thick blond hair on top of her head. "I'd rather be making the most of a spa treatment."

"You can make your own spa treatment tonight," Lily said. "Mud bath at the lake. For now, check out the view. That should help."

They all looked at the falls, not thundering like the earlier ones, but full enough. "It's pure snow melt," Lily said. "Chilly. But the water's so crystal-clear you can see to the bottom of that pool. The fish are huge."

"I can't see them from here," Jack said.

"We'll see them up close and personal tonight." Lily glanced apologetically at Michelle. "Sorry."

Michelle just shook her head, and closed her eyes. "No problem. Except this ground is hard. I hope the beds are softer."

"Um…your bed is your sleeping bag," Lily told her.

"Oh." Michelle sighed again. "Right." She looked at Jack. "I'm guessing this vacation was cheaper than last year's Italy, huh?"

"But that was then."

"What does that mean?"

"It means, time for us to learn to spend only what we make."

"We…or me?"

Jack sighed. "Okay, you."

"That's fine for you. You like camping."

"If you try," Jack said with the patience of a saint, "you might like it, too."

Michelle nodded. "Maybe. Are you going to keep me warm tonight?"

Jack blinked. "Uh…yeah. If you want me to. You haven't…"

"It might help me enjoy the experience."

"Really?"

When Michelle slowly nodded, Jack let out a hopeful smile. "Yeah. I'll keep you warm."

Jared tried not to invade their privacy, but he thought it'd be nice to have someone to keep him warm at night. He looked at Lily and found her gaze on him.

Was she thinking the same thing?

Damn hard to tell, but then she nibbled on her lower lip as if suddenly unsettled, and time seemed to stutter to a halt.

Then Rock came skidding back into camp, face pale. "It's Rose."

Lily leapt back up to her feet. "What about her?"

Rock lifted his hand, from which dangled Rose's mini skirt and halter top.

Everyone gasped.

"She went skinny dipping," Rock said. "She jumped into the falls."

"Oh my God!" Michelle cried, whipping around to look down at the water.

The river wasn't wild or rough, but it wasn't exactly low or smooth either.

"She's probably dead," Michelle said, horrified.

Lily turned to face Rock. "Show me where she jumped."

Everyone ran after them, stopping short at where Rose had dropped her shoes. They stared down at the falls, at the rock below it, and beyond that, the churning river as it flowed with shocking speed along its merry way.

Then, before Jared could grasp Lily's intentions, she toed off her shoes.

"Everyone stay here," she demanded. "Do not, and I repeat *do not,* go into the water."

And then, in a fascinating show of courage, she dove in.

6

IN DISBELIEF, Jared ran to the very edge of the cliff, his arms flapping to keep him from falling over in his rush.

She was gone.

Gone.

As he watched in horror, a screaming—and naked—Rose appeared, then just as fast, disappeared over the second falls and into the river below.

Lily surfaced in the first pool, tossing her hair and water from her face as she searched around her.

Letting out his pent-up breath, Jared cupped his hands around his mouth. "Lily! She went over the second falls!" he yelled, pointing.

Nodding, she swam toward the second waterfall.

Jesus. No one admired bravery more than him, because bravery had been what had gotten him through the past year. Well, that and a healthy fear of dying, but that was another story.

Lily had guts in spades, and it fascinated him. *She* fascinated him. "Wait here," Jared told everyone else, and took off on the trail, heading back down.

Because down was the way a screaming Rose was headed, and Lily would be right after her.

He intended to be there as well.

THE WATER closed over Rose's head and her first thought was, *uh-oh*.

Then she was caught in the current, which carried her over the second waterfall, tumbling her head over heels, again and again, until she couldn't decide which way was up and which was down, and her next thought was *Oh shit, now I've done it*.

Yeah. Jumping had seemed like a fun adventure to have, but maybe she could have thought this out a little better.

Too bad thinking ahead wasn't her strong suit. Just ask her ex-husband. If it had been, she wouldn't be here…camping. But she'd been bored at work selling second homes to rich techies in the Bay Area, tired of flirting—and sleeping with—the same techies. She wanted to mix things up a bit, and going on an outdoor adventure had seemed like a good idea.

Given the way Rock looked at her, it had been a great idea.

She wanted him. She wanted to play with him for the duration, then say bye-bye and walk away.

Her specialty.

Walk when the magic fades, and you could never get hurt. She liked that, she thought, kicking to the surface and opening her eyes. Oh my God, the sky was a sharp blue, the rest of the landscape a glorious green-and-brown blur—

Blur.

Oh, shit, the river was moving fast, and because she was in it, so was she.

Definitely not her best move. She grabbed for a branch, and missed. Two tries later she managed to grab onto a loose one. Shoving her hair out of her eyes, she surveyed the situation. She was naked in a rushing river, holding onto a branch that didn't feel all that stable, and shore seemed pretty damn far away.

So where the hunks were when she needed them? Jack with his quick smile, even if that smile was mostly directed at his sweet, spoiled wife. Jared with that laid-back, easy-going wit that was somehow much sexier than muscles, though he had those, too... Unfortunately for her, he hadn't taken his gaze off Lily since they'd started this hike. Mostly, she hoped for Rock, because he had a body meant for nibbling, and eyes that made her melt, eyes that spent a gratifying amount of time glued to her ass, but at this point—that being she was getting cold and the branch had just cracked ominously—she'd take any of them.

Leaning back, she let the sun beam down on her face and her breasts, and that felt good. She supposed she could just hang on and sunbathe for a few—

Crack went the branch, and broke.

LILY WENT OVER the second falls, plunging beneath the surface, held there for an interminably long moment by a vicious current.

Pain blossomed through her body, each muscle screaming in protest at the activity.

It'd been a while since she'd swum in pure snowmelt,

and she was less than thrilled at doing it now as the cold seeped into her newly repaired bones, making them stiff, leaving them hurting like hell.

She was going to kill Rose, if the river didn't do it first.

Kicking to the surface in the deep river, she gulped in air as she searched around her for the other woman. It wasn't hard to find her, she simply followed the sudden scream echoing and bouncing off the rock canyon walls.

Lily sped up her stroke toward the sound. *Why couldn't people follow directions?*

Then the scream abruptly cut off.

Oh, God.

Heart in her throat, Lily whipped around a curve in the river, nearly decapitating herself on a fallen log.

But then she was treading water, in shock as she focused on Jared—not where she'd left him and told him to stay, but on the river's edge—holding a naked Rose in his arms.

Obviously he hadn't listened to her any more than Rose had, an epidemic today, which really pissed her off. He'd clearly run back down the trail—at the speed of light if he'd gotten here that quick—and had jumped into the river to save the screaming, misbehaving Rose himself.

Rose practically climbed up Jared's body to glue herself against him tighter than shrink wrap. "Thank you, thank you, thank you," she was saying over and over, kissing his face, still bare-ass naked, mind you, with breasts she'd most definitely not been born with bouncing all over the place.

Jared, not seeming to mind, sank to the ground, his arms full. He'd lost his glasses and was squinting like crazy when he lifted his head and looked over at Lily with a smile. "Got her."

Yeah, she could see that. She wouldn't have guessed he'd have the strength for it, but he'd proven her wrong. He'd probably laugh, and say she was judging a book by its cover again, and she'd definitely have to agree.

She was going to have to start redefining what she saw as strength.

It definitely didn't have to come from muscles.

Gritting her chattering teeth, she began to swim to the edge, her body protesting by shooting pain through every inch. The current was a bitch, and she could definitely see how Rose had gotten herself in trouble. She was breathing like a misused racehorse herself, though a good part of that was adrenaline.

And temper.

Oh, and *pain*.

Setting her feet down, she made her way out of the water. Jared looked at her as he tried, unsuccessfully, to pull Rose's arms from his neck.

Probably Rose was practically strangling him. *Good.* "What if you'd fallen in, too?" she asked, collapsing exhausted to the shore before he could see she was trembly. "I'd still be out there, trying to save both of you."

"You're welcome." Jared had either dropped his outer shirt before he'd jumped in, or he'd lost it in the water. He pulled off the T-shirt that was clinging to his every inch, tugging it over his head with the one easy motion that guys were so good at, and then handed it to Rose.

"It's wet," Rose said in a voice that said she wasn't thinking about the wet shirt so much as his bare chest, which she was now practically lapping up.

"It's a cover," Jared pointed out, standing there just a little bit attitude-ridden and a whole lot more tough and less skinny than Lily had thought.

Like Rose, she took a second look.

And okay, maybe a third and a fourth, because, um, wow.

With a low oath, Jared tried to stuff Rose into his T-shirt himself. He was blinking rapidly, and without his glasses, still squinting.

Lily watched him shove Rose's arms into the sleeves, wondering why the hell she cared if he had to touch Rose's nude and extremely gorgeous, lush body to do it.

Because she absolutely did not care.

Not one little bit.

Nope, she had other things to worry about, thank you very much. Things such as the fact that for the first time, she'd come close to losing someone on her watch. What did that say about her ability to do this? Not much. Shoving her hair out of her face, she put her hands on her hips. "And what the hell was that, Rose? The taking-off-your-clothes-and-jumping-off-a-cliff thing?"

Rose smoothed down the T-shirt that now covered her to mid-thigh, clinging to every inch of her curvy body as if she'd just been in a wet T-shirt contest. "Yeah, sorry. That got a little crazy."

"A *little?*"

She shrugged. "The water looked so inviting."

"You might have gotten Jared killed." The thought made Lily's blood run cold, and she whirled on him as well. "And you…"

He blinked some more.

"I told you to stay."

"Again, you're welcome," he said, squinting adorably.

"Damn it, your glasses. Did you lose them?" That was all she needed, him half blind for the next four days.

"No, they're fine. I dropped them at the top with my pack." He shook his head like a dog, and water droplets showered around him. He shoved his fingers through the short mop, but all that accomplished was to make the dark ends stand straight up.

Jack and Rock came running into the clearing then, having clearly made their way down the path. In Rock's hands were Rose's clothes, and he skidded to a stop in front of her, panting, sweating, utterly speechless at the sight of her in Jared's wet T-shirt.

Apparently knowing exactly how stop-traffic-amazing she looked, and probably having caused more than her fair share of speechlessness before, Rose patted his arm in understanding and sympathy. Yeah, she seemed to be used to making men into stupid blathering idiots. "Thanks, sugar." She winked at him as she stepped into her mini skirt and shimmied it up her hips. "Sweet of you."

Lily looked up both sets of falls to where she could just make out Michelle's outline, undoubtedly anxious.

Not necessarily for Rose's health, but her own, because she wouldn't like to be alone.

Not that she'd risk a second climb back up the hill in order *not* to be alone. No, staying up there by herself was apparently the lesser of two evils. "All right," Lily said wearily. "Let's get back up to our stuff. We'll just camp there for the night and regroup." And take a bottle of ibuprofen. "Start fresh—" she looked at Rose "—and *dry,* in the morning."

Rose had the good grace to look chagrined. "Yeah. Sorry about that, honey." She snuggled into poor Rock for some of his body warmth, making his expression go from worry to looking as if he'd won the lotto.

Lily sighed. She'd known coming into this thing that this group had little wildness experience and she'd taken them on anyway. It was fine, it was her job to show them a good time out here, and she loved doing that.

And in four days they would be gone out of her life, and she'd be onto a new group. That was the beauty of this job, everything being so temporary—but she had the unsettling feeling that maybe, just maybe, temporary no longer suited her. "Let's go." She led the way back, stopping along the way at the four men sitting on the edge of the river fishing. They were the first people they'd seen all day, and they had a full bucket of trout with them. For an easy price, Lily negotiated dinner—five trout she could cook to go along with the pasta she had in her gear.

She led her group back up the winding path, dripping water on the switchbacks as she carried the fish. She was in good pain now, and didn't glance back.

She knew the men would make sure Rose got back up the hill just fine.

Honestly. Men were so stupid, letting themselves be led around by their penises. Thank God she was female.

"Hey."

She heard Jared, but kept walking, wringing water out of her braid rather than have it drip down her back and chill her further.

"Hey," he said again, and grabbing her arm, pulling her around to face him.

"Don't worry," she said, lifting the trout. "I promise they won't be slimy."

His mouth quirked at the reference to his list of things to do. His hair was still standing straight up, and at some point today he'd gotten quite a bit of sun, which had bronzed his cheekbones.

He had his shirt back from Rose, but it was wadded in his hand and not on his dry torso, so she couldn't stop her gaze from taking itself on a happy little tour, skimming over his shoulders, which were broader than she'd have guessed, and his chest, which had just the right amount of hair, not too much and not too little.

Not that she noticed.

Good Lord. Had she bumped her head in the dive? What other reason could there possibly be for her gaze to dip even farther and lock on his belly?

Flat and ridged, it rose and fell from the exertion of the tough walk.

And then there were his jeans.

God, she was a sucker for a man in jeans, and these were still wet and just loose enough that they'd slipped low, dangerously low actually, on his narrow hips, gaping away from his abs with every breath he took.

A woman, if she was so inclined, could slip her entire hand down into that loose waistband and—

"I didn't realize this had turned into a race back up to the top," he said.

"Sorry."

Reaching out, Jared slid his hand along her jaw, lifting her face, which he then frowned into, his gaze locked on her cheekbone.

"What?" She slapped his hand away.

His lips curved slightly. "You just also have a—"

"What?"

He waggled a finger, pointing to her face, then reaching in—

"I'm fine."

"Yeah, and on that, I'm completely one hundred percent in agreement, but you have a little…" Looking into her eyes, smiling, he pulled something off her cheek. A leaf, probably stuck there with dirt as well.

She swiped at her face, groaning when his smile widened. "I just smeared dirt around, right?"

"If it helps, you look extremely cute with it on your face."

Extremely cute? She didn't know quite how to take that. Hell, she didn't know how to take him. Half the time he made her want to smile, the other half of the time he made her yearn and burn for some nameless thing… Ack, the man made her crazy. Unable to come up with any kind of reasonable response, Lily turned and began walking again.

"Are you okay?" he asked, keeping pace with her.

"Why?"

He was quiet a moment. "Your limp, it's more pronounced."

"I'm good." And to prove it, she sped up. At the top of the hill, she ordered Rose and Jared to change while she made camp and got everyone settled. This involved getting a fire going so she could get a now-chilled Rose warm again. As always now with a fire, she stared into the flames and felt a creepy, unwanted flashback to another fire, one that had almost cost her everything, but she beat that back. This wasn't a campfire made by some reckless idiot. She knew what she was doing, and there would be no falling asleep until it was as out as it could be.

No flare ups.

"What about bears?" Michelle asked nervously, her teeth chattering along with Rose's. "Th-think bears'll find us?"

Jared pulled something out of his pocket. That PDA again. With a couple of taps of his thumb, he looked up. "No bears in the vicinity," he promised, and showed them the screen. It was a global positioning satellite, complete with a heat-seeking system. "It'd tell us if something alive was around here breathing."

Nothing was lit up in their vicinity but the six of them.

"Wow," Michelle said. "I want one of those."

Jared shook his head. "Prototype." He glanced at Lily, who was feeling torn between extreme irritation at his toys, and the fact that it had actually seemed to ease Michelle's mind.

With the fire crackling, and Rose hunched in front

of the flames, Lily put Rock on Rose's tent detail, which thrilled him.

Too bad he had no idea what he was doing, and she had to help him. And then Michelle and Jack as well.

After that, she turned to help Jared, assuming that he, like the others, would have no idea how to erect his tent despite the fact that they'd been given their equipment days ago with directions to practice and become proficient.

Only, once again, he managed to surprise her. His tent was already erected, and as she watched, he came out of it, walking directly behind her to set something on her shoulders.

A large towel.

"What's this?" she asked.

He tugged playfully on her hair and slid an arm around her, sharing his body heat. "You made sure everyone else changed and got warm, but you never did. You're still wet." His hands slid down her shoulders along her arms, big and warm as he gently squeezed, sharing that warmth with her.

"I'm fine," she said.

"We've already agreed that you are as fine as they come."

His voice tended to do something funny to her belly, and it tightened. Was she... *no*. She was absolutely not lusting.

Oh, God, but she was.

He ran his hands back up her arms, and she actually shivered again.

Definitely lusting. *Big-time.*

"See," he murmured in her ear, his jaw brushing hers, making her eyes want to flutter closed in order to savor the sensation. "You *were* cold."

"No," she said. A lie, of course. *Just try me,* she'd said to Keith, and now she wanted to say that very thing to Jared.

Just try me...

When he flashed a quick grin that she could feel against her skin, she could have kicked herself.

Because she'd just admitted it wasn't a chill making her shiver, but *him.*

Oh, boy. She'd wanted to claim her life again, and she was. Only she was beginning to discover she was getting much more than she'd bargained for.

She clamped her mouth shut tight so she couldn't inadvertently give anything else away. But it was too late, and he laughed softly. "So if you're not cold..." His voice was lower now, husky...pleased. "Then it's *me* making you shiver."

Nope.

Not saying a word here, not a single one, not when her brain had so clearly disconnected from her mouth.

His lips skimmed over her skin, in that delicate, oh-so-sensitive spot just beneath her lobe, and damn it, she shivered again.

"I'm tired, that's all," she said quickly to negate it. "And sore from the dive and swim."

"Need me to kiss you all better?" he whispered in a voice hot enough to set the surrounding trees on fire. "Because it worked last time..."

7

JARED WAITED, his mouth a mere breath from Lily's soft, silky skin. God, she was something, standing there so tough, so fiercely independent, so utterly arousing.

And unexpectedly sweet.

He knew her now, or was beginning to, and he wanted her more than ever.

"Do I *need* you to kiss me all better? No." Tilting her head, she met his gaze straight on, no wavering, no hiding, not for this woman. "Do I want you to? Yes. Because want is entirely different from need."

Turning her to fully face him, he smiled. "I'll take the want for now." He would earn the need, for later.

Never before had he made time to be in the middle of nowhere, doing nothing but walking and enjoying the sights for four days. And he sure as hell hadn't made time to have a wet, sexy-eyed woman stare up at him, flirt with him.

Him.

The sheer pleasure of that had a grin splitting his face. Before he'd gotten sick, he'd thought his life complete. He'd have sworn to it. But now that he was no longer consumed by either work or pain, he knew how wrong he'd been.

"It's not going to happen," she warned. "Not here. Not now." Having said so, she backed up a step, and came directly up against a tree.

Ah, wasn't that perfect. Shamelessly using the situation to his advantage, he shifted forward, gently pressing her to the trunk. Knowing he was now blocking her from the others, he set his hands on either side of her head and leaned in.

She slapped a hand to his chest. "Did you miss the not-here, not-now part?" she asked, cool as rain.

No, he hadn't missed a thing when it came to her, but fact was, her eyes had softened, gone all sleepy-lidded and dreamy, and her mouth— God, her mouth had opened slightly, her tongue touching one corner as she stared at his lips. Body language was definitely conflicting with her words, and he figured body language stood for more.

Or so he hoped.

He shifted forward another inch, and then it was that heart-stopping beat right before the kiss, the beat where they both knew it was going to happen… His eyes wanted to drift shut so that he could sink into the feel of her, the scent of her, but she kept hers open, even as he closed the distance and touched his lips to hers. He'd never kissed with his eyes open before, and it was oddly, shockingly intimate.

Then, still watching him from those whiskey eyes, she slowly sank her teeth into his bottom lip, and held on. Not deep enough to really hurt, but not exactly gentle either.

And he went instantly hard. "Uh—"

Her teeth tightened, and when he winced, her tongue

darted out and stroked his lip before she pulled back and looked at him with a cocked brow.

"Okay, so you meant it," he said on a laugh. he'd never wanted to laugh while so aroused before. "Not here, not now."

She smiled. "I just love teaching new things." With that, she tightened the towel—his towel—around her shoulders and brushed past him to check on the others.

Standing still, he watched her go, watched as she jumped right back into being in charge as if she hadn't just thoroughly rocked his world, so much so that he was going to have to stand here for a few moments before anyone got a good look at him.

One thing about no longer being consumed by work, he had the time to absorb things. Rock was showing Rose how to raise the screen on her tent's window, which faced...surprise surprise...Rock's tent.

Michelle had pulled something out of her backpack, and from here it looked like a large chocolate bar. Jack shook his head, but when Michelle broke off a piece and handed it to him, he looked at her, smiled. She smiled back as he popped it into his mouth and held out his hand for another.

Lily hunkered in front of the fire, poking at it with a stick. In less than ten seconds she had that fire leaping back to life.

And watching all this, it occurred to Jared—as he stood there waiting for the blood to circulate back into vital areas of his body, say his brain—that everyone here was consumed by something. Work, food, love...

Not him. Nope, for the first time in his life, he was

no longer consumed by anything, and it felt odd. Like the-loss-of-a-limb odd. He needed something new to get excited about, something other than work or family, something that was healthy, and soul-rewarding.

Lily rose and bent over the backpacks, pulling out supplies and food for dinner. Her still-wet cargo shorts clung to her features, her best feature right in bull's-eye view as she rifled through the packs.

And he knew. He'd found his something new—he'd found her: his enigmatic, fearless, gorgeous, sexy guide. Yeah, that so worked for him.

He only hoped it worked for her.

LILY SERVED trout over linguini for dinner, and considered the night a success when she had everyone around the campfire singing silly songs, toasting marshmallows and laughing.

Well, almost everybody. Michelle wasn't singing, she was sitting in that bright yellow rainjacket, barefoot, staring morosely at her feet. As Lily watched, Jack came close with a fistful of Band-Aids, and kneeled at her side.

Michelle pulled her feet in and shook her head.

She didn't want help, or at least not *his* help.

Jack patiently reached for one of her feet and inexorably pulled it toward him, turning it this way and that, inspecting it. Then he began opening Band-Aids and fixing her up.

Michelle tried to hold onto her frown, and managed for a good long time, but somewhere between her right and her left foot, the frown faded, and she sighed her husband's name.

"Shh," Jack said.

And just like that, the frown was back. "Why do you always shush me?"

"I don't."

"You do, you always do. I embarrass you."

Jack looked around, caught Lily looking at them, and hunched his shoulders. "When you pick a fight in public, you do."

"What do you care what anyone else thinks? I don't want you to care what anyone else thinks."

"And I, for once, would like to be able to have a discussion without yelling."

"Who's yelling?"

"You."

"I'm talking loud, I'm passionate. Excuse me."

Jack sighed and shook his head when Michelle snatched the bandages and hobbled toward their tent.

Alone.

Lily watched Jack walk off into the woods as a result, and it was her turn to sigh. Making sure that everyone was having a good time wasn't always the hard part, sometimes the people were the hard part.

And this time, unlike on any other expedition she'd ever led, she had a distraction—she was attracted to one of her group.

And not just an oh-gee-he's-cute attraction, or an I-wanna-jump-his-bones attraction.

But something much, much deeper.

Luckily she'd come to her senses.

Not before he'd kissed you...

Shaking her head over that, she decided it was time

for dishes. She took two pots and walked to one of the creeks that ran into the falls. Hunkered at the water's edge, she caught a movement out of the corner of her eye. She wasn't alone. Two masked bandits watched her very carefully—raccoons. "Sharing the water hole tonight, boys," she said softly, and reminded herself to make sure the food was locked up tight and safe, because she didn't want a bigger unwelcome guest later—a foraging, hungry bear. Rising, she turned, then gasped at the tall, dark shadow right in front of her.

"Hey," Jared said softly, his glasses reflecting the starlight from above. "Didn't meant to startle you."

"You didn't."

He kindly didn't point out that she'd nearly swallowed her tongue.

"What's everyone doing?" she asked, trying not to notice that he looked clean and warm and put together in a new pair of jeans and another button-down shirt opened over a sharp white T-shirt. Somehow it made her want to rumple him up, get him all dirty.

"They're telling stories at the moment. They started out with ghost stories…" Smiling, he shifted closer, then stroked a runaway strand of hair from her jaw to behind her ear, making her breath catch. "But at the moment, Rose is telling one that sounds more like 'Dear Penthouse.'"

"Oh boy." Lily thought of how Rose had looked earlier, rising out of the river, her enhanced breasts perfect, her everything perfect. Clearly, she tanned in the nude, because there hadn't been a bathing-suit line on her. Jared's hands, big and paler than Rose's skin, had showed up as he'd pulled her from the current, his hands on her hips, her belly, his arm wrapped around her, plumping up those breasts that didn't need plumping.

What had he thought about as he'd had those hands all over her?

Jared tipped up her chin and looked into her eyes, stepping even closer, so that they were toe to toe. All around them came that extraordinary silence that wasn't really silence at all. Trees rustling, the water gurgling, the hum of a thousand invisible insects...wildlife... With a small smile, he kept his fingers on her and made her forget all of it, everything but him.

"You're looking at me as if I might bite," he said, "when we both know it's you who bites."

She laughed. "Sorry."

"Are you?"

"Not so much, no."

Now he laughed. "I love it out here."

There was just enough surprise in his voice to have her taking a second look at him. "Why does that surprise you?"

"I didn't know what to expect. But out here, in the mountains..." He looked around them into the night. "It's different than being at sea level. You can breathe deeper, you know?"

Yeah. Yeah, she did know, and she found herself fascinated that he did, too. "What else?" she whispered.

"Well..." He considered. "The dirt's dirtier. The water's clearer. The wildflowers are brighter. It's like...I don't know, time moves differently. Better. It's worth more, here somehow."

She was so moved that he got it, it took her a moment to say anything. "I've never heard it described quite that way before."

He looked at her, his gaze open and honest, yet somehow enigmatic, as well, and she had to turn away. Above them, the stars were scattered across the sky like a million fireflies. It was mesmerizing, but truthfully? So was he. Completely. She could get lost in him, even pull him down to the ground...

He was looking at the sky, as well, and only when she turned back to him did he crane his head toward her, patient. Waiting.

"What?"

"I was wondering what you were thinking about," he said.

"Nothing. I wasn't thinking about anything."

"Liar," he chided softly. "Tell me."

She gestured to the two pots. "I need to get this stuff put away and check on the others—"

He pulled her up. "Talk to me, Lily."

"Today when you saved Rose—"

"I didn't save her."

"You helped her. She might have gone a lot farther down the river if you hadn't."

He acknowledged that with a shrug, and pushed his glasses farther up his nose.

Modest. She hadn't spent a lot of time with men like Jared Skye. In fact, she'd spent most of her time with men his exact opposite, on purpose, though now she wondered why. There was definitely something to be said for such quiet strength.

Maybe it was because when it came right down to it, she knew she could resist a cocky guy. She could keep her heart locked up tight as a drum.

But not necessarily with a man like Jared, whose strength came from within.

Oh boy, those were deep thoughts, far too deep for right now with the woods around them dark and silent, making this little gathering too intimate for her tastes.

"Is that really what you were thinking about?" he asked.

She didn't intend to look into his eyes, but she felt the pull of him like that of the tide, or the need for her next breath.

His gaze was dark, but not guarded. Nope, everything he felt was right there on his sleeve for the world to see.

She'd spent her entire life moving around, shifting from one profession to another, free as a bird. And yet it was all an illusion, she realized, because for as free as she'd been, she'd never been truly open with her feelings.

Though the night was moonless, she could see Jared with shocking clarity, or maybe that was because he stood so damn close. His shoulders were surprisingly wide, wide enough for her to set her head on and let go of her troubles if she chose. And though she had no idea how he managed such a feat, he smelled incredible. Her nose twitched pathetically. She wanted to inhale him. "You got me," she finally admitted. "I was thinking of other stuff, too."

"Like...?"

Like kissing you.

Like dropping to my knees and touching you. Having you touch me.

As if he could read her mind, his fingers stroked her jaw, held her face so that he could see deep into her eyes. "Lily."

Oh God. That voice. It made her want to do things. It made her want *him* to do things.

To her.

"I'm going to be honest with you," she said.

"Uh-oh."

She shook her head. "This is my first expedition after a tough year, and I need my wits about me. But when I look at you, my wits scatter."

He flashed a grin.

She shook her head with a laugh. "No. Don't do that. Because I'm going to resist you, Jared Skye. With all my might."

"Where's the fun in that?"

"I'm serious."

"Okay."

"You're not even my type," she said, still baffled by this. "Not even close."

"Huh." He cocked an eyebrow. "What's your type?"

"Oh…" She winced. "Well…"

"Just say it, Lily." A wry smile curved his lips. "More of an outside guy, right?"

She thought of how he'd run down the trail after Rose with the agility of a mountain cat. How he'd waded into the river without thought to his own safety. Seemed fairly "outside" to her, didn't he? Damn, she'd been so sure she'd had him pegged.

"Maybe someone with..." With what? More sex appeal? Not possible, because she was beginning to realize he had sex appeal in spades. "Damn it. I don't know."

He nodded but didn't back up, didn't get out of her space, and truthfully, she wasn't all that ready to have him move, no matter what she'd said.

"It'd be good between us," he said.

Oh, yeah. She knew that much. Turning from temptation—him—she faced the tree and set her forehead to it. "I don't even know you."

"Yes, you do. Or you're starting to."

"I don't know you well enough."

"And you like to know a guy."

No. No, she didn't like to know a guy, thank you very much. She was more of a one-night-stand girl if the truth was going to be told.

Which it wasn't.

He put his hands on her hips and turned her back around, holding her gaze in his while she felt his hand cover hers on her thigh, which she'd been unconsciously rubbing.

"You're hurting," he murmured.

"No, I'm fine—"

"I have some ibuprofen—"

"I'm *fine*." Humiliated that she hadn't hidden it, that he'd been able to so thoroughly see right through her to the things she hadn't wanted anyone to see, she tried to twist free, but he held her still, studying her face carefully.

"You think of it as a weakness," he said in disbelief. "Your injury."

"It *is* a weakness. I'm your guide, I'm not supposed to be whining about a little residual pain."

Putting his hands on her shoulders, he turned her back to face the tree again. Then he lifted her hands to the trunk and pressed gently, signaling that she was supposed to stay like that, just where he put her.

No one ever got to tell her what to do, and yet he did, and she'd let him—

He dug his fingers into the muscles of her shoulders, and ohmigod, all thoughts flew right out of her head because he hit it right on the nail. His fingers moved over her muscles, coaxing out the tension, and before she could stop it, also a throaty moan that horrified her with its neediness. She clamped her lips shut tight, but he just leaned in, putting his mouth to her ear. "Relax," he said. "I'm good at this."

He wasn't kidding. She tried to relax, she really did, but she could feel his body just behind hers, not quite touching, but almost...

"Relax," he said again. Those talented fingers moved up her neck and down her back and shoulders, unbelievably pulling out the tension and relieving the pain.

Not to mention melting her bones.

Seriously, if he kept this up, she was going to slip to the floor in a boneless heap, maybe even have an orgasm. Or maybe she'd just strip and beg him to take her.

"Good?" he asked.

"You must have girls falling all over themselves with this talent," she managed.

His fingers went still for a beat, then resumed. "Yeah, I have them lining up at my door."

Tipping her head back, she looked up at him.

"I'm not exactly a babe magnet," he explained, and at her bemused look, he smiled. "Techno-geek, remember?"

"Well," she said softly, oddly touched, her voice suddenly gruff. "Women can be extremely shortsighted."

At that, his smile reached his eyes. "It doesn't help that I used to work 24-7, without time for anything else. I'm trying to fix that."

"What, being a techno-geek?"

He laughed. "Working 24-7."

Reaching up, she ran her fingers through his hair. "You know what I think? That any woman who passed you over was an idiot." Including herself.

"I pretty much fly under most women's radar."

It shamed her to know that he'd nearly flown under her radar. That she would have passed him by on the street without a second thought, shrugging him off as not her type, simply because his world was so different from hers. "Women need to be retrained from adolescence," she decided. "The bad boys? Not where it's at."

He laughed. "Yeah. Thanks." He set her hands back on the tree and resumed his incredible assault on her tense muscles, and pretty soon, she was a puddle at his feet. Another minute, or even less, and she was going to start drooling. "That's good," she managed. "Thanks."

He didn't take the hint and remove his hands from her. In fact, he kept at it until she could feel the last of her tight muscles loosen, until she could hardly remember her own name.

"Yeah, that's it," he said quietly, still massaging. "Better, huh?"

So much better that she had to lock her knees.

"You're like a rock quarry."

"I know." She felt his gaze on her, and kept silent.

He didn't. "So you fell off a cliff trying to fight an out-of-control forest fire, you nearly died, were told you'd never walk again—which you proved wrong by sheer wil—and…help me out here…you honestly think of it as something to be ashamed of."

"No."

"You do," he said, putting his hands on her hips to turn her to face him, dipping down a bit when she tried to look away. "Seriously, Lily. Life's too short for that kind of shit. Trust me. I know."

She was eye level with his throat, which just this morning had been silky smooth, fresh from a shave. Now there was a day's growth there, and suddenly he didn't seem quite so neat and tidy. "There's…something you don't know about what happened to me."

"What?"

"Before I slipped off the cliff, there'd been a fire."

"I figured that, since you were there as a firefighter."

"I was on mop-up duty. It was my job to make sure there were no flare-ups. And I fell asleep."

"You were probably exhausted."

"When I woke up, the fire had started again. That's my fault. I missed a flare-up. I screwed up big-time, Jared."

"Everyone makes mistakes, Lily."

"Yeah." She looked away. Needed to look away. "Thanks for the massage."

"But?"

She looked at him, and was caught by his wry smile. "But?"

"I'm pretty sure I heard a big but at the end of that sentence. Thanks for the massage, Jared, but you're not my type...right?"

"You're not," she reminded them both.

"Look, I'm well aware of the fact that you're totally out of my league." He let out a rough laugh. "And only six months ago I'd have had to talk myself into trying for you. A year ago I'd never have even considered it."

"Why not?"

"Because, like I said, I was an ordinary working stiff turned classic workaholic, who put in twenty-hour days, seven days a week. I was addicted to the office, to the work, to the adrenaline and excitement that comes from making money hand over fist. I wouldn't have had time even to think about going out with you."

"Why did you stop working like that?"

He looked away, a rare thing with him, and her stomach dipped, insinuating she knew, that whatever it was, it was bad. "It's okay," she whispered. "You don't have to tell me if you don't want to."

His smile was a tad crooked, and extremely endearing. "Don't really want to know, huh?"

"I just have a feeling I'm not going to like it."

"I got sick."

Her stomach dipped again. "What happened, your boss fire you for missing a few days?"

"I'm my own boss," he reminded her. "And I missed five months."

She swallowed hard past the uncomfortable lump in her throat. Yeah. Definitely bad. "That must have been a helluva sickness."

"It was cancer," he said. "And I know this sounds clichéd, but I should have died and I didn't. I cheated the Grim Reaper and because of that, I'm not the same anymore."

"Cancer?" she whispered, and found her hands clutching his arms. "Are you...did you..."

"I'm recovered, heading toward remission."

She couldn't take her hands off him, as if he might vanish if she let go, and he seemed to understand the reaction, because he let out a little smile. "I'm okay, Lily."

"Of course you are." She tried to loosen her fingers so at least she wasn't hurting him, but couldn't. He felt okay, she assured herself. Beneath her fingers he was warm and strong. "My God, Jared. You must have been through so much." She managed to let go of him to reach up and run a hand over his short, short hair.

"Yeah." His smile went a little self-conscious as he ran his fingers over it. "That's all new growth."

And just like that, right then and there, she felt her heart catch. Oh, God. That couldn't be good.

She hadn't realized that she'd put a hand over her aching heart until he took her fingers in his. "Mostly," he said. "I learned, along with the newfound humility, and how much being sick sucks, that life is damn precious. I missed too much of it, Lily. No more."

She couldn't tear her eyes off him either. More, she found she had to hear him say it again. "You're...fine though. *Right?*"

"Very," he assured her.

Still staring at him, she let out a long breath. "Okay. Okay, then." She breathed some more. "Wow. That word sort of just grabs you by the throat. *Cancer.*"

"Not many people actually use the word in front of me," he admitted. "I hate that."

"Cancer." She fisted both hands in his shirt. "Cancer. It's just a word, not so scary, right?"

He smiled, and cupped her face. "I'm really okay, Lily."

She resisted the childish urge to make him promise. "So…it changed you."

"You saw my list."

"Yes." And now the significance of it made so much more sense.

"I wrote it on the day I decided not to die."

She wanted to flinch from that word, but refused, for him. She imagined him in the hospital, writing that list, not sure if he was going to live to do those things on it. It grabbed her by the throat and held tight. To combat it, she bent for the two pots she'd cleaned in the river.

"Actually," he said. "I've thought of a new addition to the list."

"What's that?"

He smiled and nudged her backwards against the tree again. "To be with a fiercely independent, prideful, tough as hell, prickly, oblivious-to-her-own-appeal woman."

"Jared—"

"You, Lily." His gaze dropped to her mouth. "I want to be with you."

She felt her insides melt away. She'd been so busy trying to be strong, and had always wanted a guy with that same obvious strength. But here the quiet, easy-going guy had turned out to be the one with the strength—the inner strength.

And it was more arousing than any show of muscles had ever been. "By *be with,* you mean—"

"Well, this for starters."

And pressing her up against the rough bark, he kissed her, long and hard and wet, and ohmigod, like he was never going to let her go, and at the moment, that worked for her, it really worked.

8

KISSING LILY was like…well, Jared didn't really know because there was nothing like it. *Nothing*. He experienced the unique, rushing thrill of hearing her drop the two pots at her feet, as if she couldn't concentrate on both his mouth and a single other thing.

Oh, yeah, he liked that.

And then there was the way her hands came up and sank in his barely-there hair, tight, like maybe she didn't want him to get away until she was completely finished with him.

Ditto.

God. Her lips had been a little chilled at their first touch but they warmed quickly beneath his.

Another thrill.

As was the feel of her tongue as it slid to his. Definitely he could drown in her, just let himself go right under, and, happily doing just that, he leaned into her, a move that sandwiched her between the tree and his own body, pressing her snugly against him. His hands free, he slid them up her body, groaning at the hot, tight feel of her, and given the sexy little sounds that escaped her throat, she was drowning, too.

Never coming up for air, he thought, never, and frustrated by the layers between them, he slid his hands beneath her shirt to find warm, silky skin. Oh yeah—

A scream shattered the night, and they both jerked free.

"Shit," Lily gasped, and shoving her shirt back down, went running back into camp, with him right on her heels.

They skidded into the clearing around the campfire, taking in the situation. It looked as if everyone had dropped whatever they were doing to rush over to Jack's and Michelle's tent, including Jack, who was now holding a sobbing Michelle.

"What happened?" Lily demanded, after pushing in front of Rose and Rock.

Everyone started talking at once, including Jack, but Lily held up her hand. "Wait. Michelle?"

Michelle hiccupped and kept her face buried in Jack's T-shirt.

Jack rolled her eyes, and at the movement, Jared sensed Lily relax. If Jack was annoyed, then Michelle wasn't dying.

Probably.

"Michelle," Lily said, dropping to her knees besides them. "Talk to me."

"A spider," she gulped, tightening the fisted grip she had on Jack's shirt, making him wince. "A big, fat, hairy, humungous spider!"

"Okay." Lily glanced back at Jared, but somehow managed to keep a straight face. "There are a lot of spiders out here, we're in their territory."

Michelle shook her head. "You've got to get it out of there!"

Jack sighed. "Michelle."

Lily patted the sobbing Michelle on the back. "Listen, don't make yourself sick. Where's the spider?"

"On my pillow! I'm never going to sleep on that pillow again!"

"So I carted it seven miles up this mountain for nothing?" Jack asked.

Michelle pushed him away from her. "This is not a time for jokes, Jack."

"Who was joking?"

Lily ignored both of them to duck into the tent. She reappeared a moment later.

"Your hands are empty," Michelle said, her voice tight with panic. "Lily, your hands are empty."

"It's gone," Lily said regretfully.

"Probably your screaming scared him off— *What?*" Jack asked when Michelle stopped crying to smack him. "That's a good thing, right?"

"I think so," Lily said, nodding. "A really good thing."

Jared glanced down at the door of the tent. "Hey. Look." He grabbed a stick and nudged the indeed big, black, fat, hairy spider onto it. "Got him."

Michelle screamed again and buried her face against her husband's chest.

"I'll take it into the woods," Jared said quickly, and moved to the far edge of camp. By the time he'd turned back, Michelle had a new horror—the chances that the spider had laid babies in her tent.

"Doubtful," Lily was saying. "Very doubtful."

"Doubtful, but possible, right?"

Lily shook her head. "They don't lay babies at night." She said this with an utterly straight face.

Jack nodded his agreement. "That's right. I read that somewhere."

"Yeah?" Michelle rounded on him. "Where did you read it?"

Rock stepped forward. "Look, you guys can switch tents with me."

Jack shook his head. "That's not necessary—"

"Thank you," Michelle said gratefully, and with a scathing look at her husband, stalked off toward Rock's tent.

Jack sighed. "Sorry," he said to Rock, who shrugged.

"No sweat."

"We should all get to bed," Lily said into the silence. "We have an early start tomorrow morning, so we all need to sleep tight—"

"And not let the bedbugs bite," Jack joked, only to have Michelle whirl back in horror from Rock's tent.

"Just kidding," he said. "Just kidding!" And he headed to his new tent for the night.

When it was just Lily and Jared, she looked at him. "It's getting to be that maybe I should get you on the payroll for this expedition."

"It was just a spider removal."

"A timely one."

"No big deal." He shrugged, and watched a lizard dart beneath a manzanita bush at the edge of the fire. "Hope she doesn't see *that* little guy."

"She's bound to see plenty of things she doesn't like." She didn't come any closer, he noted. Because she didn't trust herself? He sort of liked the thought of that.

"Thanks," she said. "For tonight."

"No thanks required. But if you want to be grateful…"

Her smile went just a little guarded when he stepped around the fire to get closer.

"Jared."

"Don't say it was a mistake," he said quietly, and they both knew they were no longer talking about the spider.

"Not a mistake," she said. "Just not wise."

"Then why did it feel so good?"

"Good doesn't always equal right. Look…" She turned in a slow circle, clearly searching for words. "I've always tried to be in charge of my destiny, you know?"

"So?"

"So, right now my destiny is kicking me in the ass."

"Because you can't be a firefighter?"

"Because I don't know what I want to be." She tossed up her hands. "Or who I am. I came here to try to start over, back at the beginning, to try to figure it all out." At that, she shook her head. "And I have no idea why I tell you such things."

"Because it's a natural fit between us."

"A natural fit?" She frowned. "That makes it sound like we're a thing."

He smiled.

"Oh, no." With a little laugh, she shook her head. "No *thing.*"

"We kissed," he reminded her. "That felt like a thing, a big one."

She shook her head again. "I don't know why I kissed you."

"I know." He cupped her jaw for the sheer pleasure of touching her again. "I don't know what exactly what it is about you either. But I'm willing to find out." He looked into her beautiful eyes. "And as for you not knowing who you are, you'll figure it out."

She stared up at him. "Have you always been so self-assured, always known exactly who you are?"

At that, he laughed. Had he always known? Try never—until recently.

"I take that as a no."

"A hell no," he corrected. "I grew up a small, skinny, sickly, self-conscious nerd."

"Nerd made good," she said softly.

"It took a while. Years. And then, when it all came right down to it, none of it meant a damn. Not the success, the huge corporation, the money in the bank accounts, nothing. I couldn't have taken a thing with me."

"Except this." Surprising him, she put her hand over his heart, and he covered it with one of his own.

"You know what?" she whispered.

"What?" he whispered back, unbearably moved, wanting her to keep her hand on him all night long.

Her smile shimmered. "Every minute you spend in these mountains, you seem to lose a little bit of that city boy."

"Oh, yeah?"

"Yeah. I don't know how you're doing it…" She ran her hand up his chest, his throat, to his jaw, the pads of her fingers making a rasping sound over his day-old growth. "But you sure are tougher than I imagined when I first saw you."

Bringing her hand up to his mouth, he pressed his lips to her palm. "Know what I thought when I first saw you?"

"That I was going to steal your parking spot?" she whispered.

"Well, that, and also..." His gaze met hers. "That you were the sexiest woman I'd ever laid my eyes on."

"I was frowning at you," she reminded him.

"Ah, yes. The frown. I think that clinched it for me."

She tried to tug free. "Stop it."

He held on and smiled. "Serious. Sexiest woman ever."

"Wow." Her voice sounded a little shaken. "I think it's bedtime. 'Night, Jared." Turning away, she went still, then glanced back. "Don't let the bedbugs bite."

He knew a dismissal when he heard one. "Maybe it will make better sense in the morning."

"The bedbugs?"

"No."

Her gaze dropped to his mouth. "The kiss?"

"All of it."

"Including the reasons why we shouldn't do any of it again?"

He wanted to say the hell with that, but she'd turned away to deal with putting the fire out.

He went into his tent and lay down, surrounded by night noises that he was extremely unused to. Crickets chirped their odd song. From the hills came a lonely, edgy howl.

He knew the feeling.

Then came an answering howl, a pause, and then both of them together.

As one.

With a sigh, Jared turned over and wished it was that simple, that he could simply toss back his head and let loose with a howl and have Lily appear right here next to him. But he wasn't an animal, he was a human, and supposedly they'd evolved way past such a thing.

LILY DIDN'T SLEEP as hard as she'd have liked. First, she kept jerking awake to check on the campfire.

But she'd put it out completely, and she had nothing to worry about.

Other things though…other things kept bouncing through her head.

Jared.

Cancer.

He hadn't come right out and said it, but she knew, and it'd been bad. So bad he'd seemed just a little surprised to still be around, and if that didn't grab her by the throat and hold on tight…

But he'd made it, and she was fiercely glad and proud and overwhelmed with a newfound sense of wonder. It was far too easy to forget how fragile life could be, how short, how absolutely, stunningly beautiful.

She for one wouldn't waste the reminder, and the next morning, with thoughts of Jared, of life in general, still on her mind, she got up early.

Up at this altitude, dawn came as a rose strip where the streaked sky met the spiky black ridges. The breathtaking view wouldn't last more than a moment, but she'd lived her life by the moment, without too much thought to the past or future. She certainly didn't have a list in her pocket of things she wanted to experience.

The thought of a predetermined plan like that had always seemed completely beyond her.

But Jared had a list, and this trip was on it. That meant she was going to make sure that these four days would never be forgotten.

A little heat filled her cheeks at that, because hadn't she already maybe done that?

Oh, yes, she had.

She went to the water and took a quick bath. Then she busied her hands, and her mouth, with breakfast. As always, the scents of coffee and bacon cooking over an open fire drew everyone out of their tents, and she put a smile on her face, determined to make today a great one, spiders or skinny-dipping, or whatever came her way.

Jared showed up first, his short hair sticking straight up in classic bed head that should have looked ridiculous but somehow seemed sexily rumpled instead. In direct contrast, his sweatshirt and jeans were clean and neat, not a wrinkle anywhere to indicate that they'd been in a backpack overnight. He seemed rested and warm and just a little bit groggy, which she found even more sexy, and her brain disconnected from logic again as a small part of her wished it was just the two of them, that she could have crawled into his sleeping bag to see his eyes open on her.

Those eyes landed right on her anyway, dark and sleepy-lidded, and she wondered what he was thinking.

He didn't look away, didn't shutter his gaze, just let her see the truth—that what he was thinking about was being with her, preferably naked and writhing and sweaty, and, oh God, she had to take a deep breath and look away.

He went to the water, passing Rock, who appeared in his black gear, looking freshly clean, hair still wet. He had a hopeful expression as circled the frying pan filled with sizzling bacon. "You, Lily Peterson, are a goddess."

"Thank you," she said. "Although you should probably wait until after today's hike to see if you still feel that way. And careful," she warned as he poured himself coffee, "it's hot."

"Tough hike today, then?"

"Nothing you can't handle," she promised. "We're going to take a trail that bisects Rainbow Ridge. There's a handful of lakes only a blink away from the top. Good thing, too, 'cause we'll be wanting a swim by then. Careful," she said again as he lifted the mug to his lips. "It's—"

He hissed out a breath when he burned his tongue.

And Lily just sighed.

Rose actually poked her head out next. "Gimme," she said, honing in on the coffeepot with an eagle eye. "Gimme quick, before I remember I have no makeup on, or that there's no hair straightener in sight."

Rock rushed to give her his mug, waiting until she'd had a big gulp before he smiled at her. "You don't need makeup, Rose. Or a hair straightener."

She looked at him as she continued to sip the steaming brew. "No?"

"No way."

She looked at him some more. "Do lines like that usually work for you?"

"Lines?"

"Uh-huh." Rose took another long sip of the caffein-ated brew. "Where did you learn to sweet-talk a woman like that anyway?"

Rock blushed. "I'm not— I don't know."

Rose laughed and handed him back the mug as she climbed out of her tent, wearing low-slung shorts and another halter top. "God, how is it you're still so sweet?" She rumpled his hair. "Hasn't any woman ever screwed you over?"

"No ma'am." He tried to pretend he wasn't staring at her body. "At least, I don't think so."

On the far side of the fire, Jack backed out of his tent. Michelle followed. She looked a little worse for wear, but Jack poured her some coffee.

She looked down at the steaming brew. "No cappuc-cino right?"

Jack's mouth tightened. "Michelle—"

She laughed, the first time Lily had even heard that sound from her. "Just kidding, Jack. Jeez, lighten up."

Jack stared at Michelle until she ran a self-conscious hand over her own tousled hair. "What? Is my hair crazy? I told you—"

"No, it's just that you look so pretty when you smile."

And Michelle's smile brightened. "Really? Thanks."

Lily moved in to feed everyone. "Eat up," she said, enjoying that, for the moment at least, everyone seemed relaxed and happy. "We've got a hike to get to."

THE DAY'S six-mile hike was tough but went smoothly, and at the end of it, everyone dropped their packs and changed into their bathing suits behind the trees. Michelle, still in her yellow raingear, dragged Jack with her to "protect" her from spiders.

Lily thought she'd do better to worry about sunburn with that tiny bikini she came back in, but then Rose came out in an even smaller itty-bitty set of black strings and blinded the men.

Jared came out from behind his tree in nothing but a dark-blue pair of swim trunks that started well below his abs and fell to his knees, the CEO within him nowhere to be found—not in the two-day growth on his jaw or his finger-combed hair, and without a single piece of digital equipment on him.

He handed something to Rose and Michelle, who thanked him profusely, and then in the next moment, music filled the air.

Okay, *almost* no digital equipment on him.

"iPod," he said as he sat next to her. "They've been begging me."

"Uh-huh."

Unperturbed, Jared sighed in bliss and leaned back on his elbows. "My mom and sisters would never have wanted to hike for two days to get here, but they'd sure love this view. We did a lot of sitting at the beach in my youth."

"Sounds nice."

"Oh, sure. My sisters would bury me in the sand and force-feed me seaweed. Nice."

She laughed. "My mom didn't like to travel."

"But you do."

"Yeah, well, it's hereditary." She rolled her eyes, a

little uncomfortable with the revelation. "Got it from my father." As she had a lot of things, apparently.

"He's a guide, too?"

"Nope. A travel writer." All Lily's life she'd been told she was just like him, and all her life that had brought her a mixture of great pride and also a healthy dose of uneasiness.

"He must be proud of you."

"I wouldn't know. He only managed to stay with us until I was one. I understand that was a record for him."

"He just up and left you both?"

He sounded horrified, and after the way he'd grown up, surrounded by family and swaddled in affection, she could understand why, and felt a little pathetic. "He went to Italy," she said lightly. "Then France. I think he's in Germany now."

"Did your mom ever remarry?"

She closed her eyes and leaned back too, more comfortable when she couldn't watch him watch her. "Hard to, since she's still married to my dad. He coaxes her to him just often enough to keep her in love with him."

He was quiet a moment. "So was it just you and your mom?"

"Oh, no. She runs an inn in Santa Monica, so there were new people in and out of our lives all the time."

"My house felt like an inn with four sisters and all their friends coming and going," he said. "But really, it was always the same people all the time."

She opened her eyes. The others were sunning, swimming, having a good time. Enjoying themselves. And despite the fact she was talking about herself—never easy—so was she, she realized. Enjoying herself. "We're different, you know. As in night-and-day different."

Jared let out a slow grin. "I have to admit, some of those differences I'm grateful for."

She arched a brow at the teasing note in his voice. "Isn't it time for you to go swimming?"

"As a matter of fact, it is." Standing, he tossed his glasses to the grass and leapt into the water with an ease that told her he hadn't been all work and no play, no matter what he'd said about himself.

And she had to admit that while he looked extremely fine in his extremely fine hiking gear, he looked even finer in far less.

She had no idea what it was about him, but the tougher the going got, the more alpha he became. And the more attractive.

And sexier…

Oh, boy. She was in deep trouble here.

Rose and Michelle stretched out on the shore and slathered each other in suntan lotion. As they watched the two women do each other's backs, Rock's and Jack's tongues hung out as if they were watching a porno flick.

Jared appeared at Lily's side, dripping wet, of course, and, hunkering down, smiled into her face. "Hey."

"Hey back."

"Sun feels good, huh?"

It did, but that wasn't what went through her mind as she looked up at him. She'd managed to stay ahead of him most of the hike today, because she'd needed time to process.

But all she'd processed was this…*she wanted another yummy kiss.*

"Why don't you go in for a swim?" he asked.

"I'm not quite ready— Hey!" was all she had time to squeak when he simply bent and hoisted her up in his arms, his wet arms, arms that were far stronger than she'd given him credit for.

From above, on the rocks, Michelle and Rose laughed. Jack and Rock yelled for Jared to dunk her.

"Jared, don't be silly," Lily said quickly. "Put me down."

An evil grin flashed across his features. "Well, all right, if you say so."

And the next thing she knew, she was flying into the air, then landing with a splash into the lake.

The water closed around her.

Going to kill him, she thought, breaking the surface, just as another huge splash had her treading water and closing her eyes to the wild cheers on the shore.

Jared surfaced next to her. He shook his head like a shaggy dog and grinned at her. "Well, hello."

"I suppose you think you're funny."

"You screamed like a girl."

"Did not."

"Oh, yeah, you did," Jack yelled helpfully from the shore.

Rock, grinning, nodded.

"Our fearless leader," Jared laughed, and snagged her close. "Squealing for her life."

"I did not *squeal.*"

"Want to bet?" His eyes turned daring. "Anything. You name it."

She wouldn't take that bet. She never took sucker bets.

The water was cool, but Jared's body against hers brought a warmth that couldn't entirely be attributed to sheer physics.

He grinned, waiting her out.

Oh boy. There was chemistry involved here, plenty, and for a long moment she let her body bump up against his, belly to belly, thigh to thigh…and everything in between.

Either he was carrying something in his pocket, or he'd gotten hard. And even as she thought it, his grin slowly faded, his eyes heated. *Flamed.*

An answering shiver came from deep inside her. It'd been so long since she'd experienced the feeling, it took a moment to recognize.

Sheer, sensual, earthy, sexual anticipation.

His hands went to her hips as he treaded water, keeping them both afloat with an ease that startled her. Where was her beta-electronic-city-boy geek? She needed him to make an appearance, damn it, so that she could come to her senses.

But he was nowhere to be found. In his place was a confident, strong, easygoing alpha male whom she was finding harder and harder to resist. And speaking of hard…she nudged up against him for the sheer pleasure of feeling him again. Oh boy. *"Who are you?"* she whispered.

"Just a guy, Lily. A guy who's looking at you. Seeing you."

"Jared."

"Wanting you."

"Please," she whispered.

"Too much, too soon?"

"*Yes.*"

"Hmm. Well, that I can fix." With a flashing grin that should have been her warning, he let go of her, put a hand on her head, and dunked her.

Okay, that was it, she thought, sputtering as he just cracked up. *He was dead.*

And thus began the wildest, most fun water fight she'd ever had.

By the time it was over, they were all in the water— well, except for Michelle, who'd remained sunning on her rock—all of them having the time of their lives.

Mission accomplished, Lily thought with a pleased weariness.

And finally they dragged themselves out of the lake and onto the shore, lying there gasping for breath, happily exhausted as two monarch butterflies fluttered through the air over them, alighting on the rocks, fanning their bright orange wings.

"Ah," Rose said. "This is the life."

Jared smiled at Lily, his eyes agreeing.

Lily herself had to admit, it was nice, very nice.

And then, far above, a head appeared over the ridge, and an arm waved.

Lily sat up. Their first drop of supplies had arrived, which had been expected.

What hadn't been expected...it was Keith handling the delivery.

9

"YOU'RE LOOKING good."

Lily looked up. Keith stood a few feet away. He'd helped her cook dinner—stir fry—charming the guests in his easy way, snubbing her idea of regular chocolate chip cookies for dessert, instead brandishing what he'd brought them...black forest mousse.

Everyone had dived right on that, and he'd sent Lily a knowing smile. He loved making his people happy, and he did consider the group his.

Including, she had the feeling, herself. He made sure to touch her, a lot. He followed her to the water when she went to clean the dishes, then took over the task himself, squatting his leanly muscled frame down, scrubbing a pan with ease.

Watching him, it all came back to her. Being eighteen and inexperienced, knowing only that she'd never been given a chance to please her father, and wanting desperately to please her first employer.

Keith had loved that need in her.

She'd come here lost, looking for herself, wondering if she could go back to that woman she'd been, and possibly pick up where they'd left off.

But she was coming to realize how much she'd changed. She was no longer a young, needy girl but her own woman, a woman who rarely, if ever, let anyone else run her world.

She knew now that it couldn't work between her and Keith. What she felt for him was firmly rooted in her past, and much as she'd thought she'd wanted to, she couldn't go back.

From where he hunkered at the water's edge, he smiled up at her, that same smile that had once been her entire world. "Your back okay? You need me to stick around?"

"No. I'm...fine."

His smile remained but she felt his disappointment. He finished the pan and stood close. His sun-kissed hair was slightly disheveled, which only added to the fact that he was gorgeous. Once upon a time she'd spent hours just looking at him. Days.

Months.

"Seriously," he said softly. "You're looking good."

She knew damn well her hair was a wreck, her jeans were dirty, and that, overall, especially when compared to him, she looked like something the cat had dragged in.

She also knew he genuinely didn't care about any of that. "Thanks." She took the pans from him. Unlike at last night's camp, she was in plain sight of the tents and campfire, where the rest of the campers lounged and relaxed. Or where Rose was lounging and relaxing. Rock was doing pull-ups on a tree branch and trying not to take peeks at Rose. Michelle was giving herself a pedicure, sitting on her yellow rainjacket to keep herself off the ground and presumably spider-free. Jack and Jared had gone into the woods to get some fuel for the fire.

Jared. He hadn't said one word about Keith appearing with the supplies. She wondered if he thought she'd invited him here.

Not that it mattered what he thought.

"Being out here really agrees with you," Keith said, bringing her attention back to him as he moved close. Smiling into her face, he ran a finger over her cheekbone. "Getting some color back on you."

Used to be, his touch had melted her. Now she just wanted him to go because she hated the confusing mix of past and present. "Can I ask you something, Keith?"

"Sure."

"Do you ever think about us?"

"A lot, since you've called." He took the pans back from her. "I was thinking you had some ideas about starting up with me again."

"I did," she admitted softly. "But now I'm thinking that was stupid."

"Still say whatever comes into your head, I see." He didn't seem insulted, but amused. "I thought maybe you'd outgrow that."

"Apparently not."

"Actually, it's refreshing. There's no subterfuge with you, Lil. No guessing. It's all out there in the open for anyone to see." He laughed softly. "I wasn't mature enough to appreciate that the first time around. I hope to rectify that."

She looked into his eyes. Back then, she'd loved looking into his dark, unwavering eyes, loved guessing at his thoughts. She'd always had to guess, since he hadn't ever been good at revealing himself. "How?"

He answered with a smile and a wicked gleam.

"Do you really think it's a good idea for me to jump back into your bed?"

"Or yours. I'm not picky."

She laughed at his audacity and smooth confidence, then her smile faded. "Keith…"

His smile faded, too. "I'm not going to like this, am I?"

She took his hand. "I took the job because I was lonely and hurting and afraid I'd lost myself."

"You don't look lost to me."

"That's because being here reminds me of the woman I was back then: strong, confident, ready to take on the world."

"You were—*are,* an amazing woman."

"Keith…"

He took in her expression. "Ah, hell. I hate the truth."

"I'm not that same woman. And maybe the sooner I face that, the better."

"Maybe that's true. Maybe you're not that woman anymore, maybe you're better."

She let out a low laugh. "Better? Uh, no."

His gaze went on a slow tour of her, from head to toe, and back again, stopping at each spot in between. "You're looking just as fine as always." He looked her in the eyes, then leaned in and kissed her cheek. "And I hope you end up seeing that." With a sigh, he tipped his head back to the gorgeous night sky, lit up with the glow of a million stars. "It never gets old, that view, does it?"

"No." On this one thing at least, they were in complete agreement. "It doesn't."

"We were here once together, near this exact spot actually, beneath a night just like this." He flashed a grin. "Remember?"

Her second expedition, as a matter of fact. He'd set her up in a tent that they'd never used. Instead they'd spread out a blanket and lain beneath a sky just like this one. He'd pointed out all the constellations, telling her stories about each one, and her eighteen-year-old heart had sighed.

She'd fallen hard. "I remember."

"We were good together, Lily."

"Were."

"Ah." He nodded. "It's someone else you're thinking of now."

Jared. God, it was true. "I'm sorry."

"It's okay, Lil." His gaze went to a spot over her shoulder, and then, reaching out, he put a finger over her mouth, ran it over her lower lip in a caress. "One more then, for old time's sake." He kept his eyes locked onto hers as he slowly leaned in and kissed her.

Her first thought—he felt warm and comfortable, nothing more. Her second, and far more unsettling thought—that she could think at all meant she wasn't feeling anything close to what she'd felt when Jared had kissed her. It was shockingly simple. For Keith, she felt a mix of affection and youth, all of it firmly past tense.

In the present, right here, right now, she felt...nothing, and she pulled back. "Keith, I—"

His gaze was drifting over her shoulder, and she found that just odd enough to turn and see what it was that he kept looking at.

Jared had come back into camp. He dropped a load of wood, brushed off his hands and his shirt, but even with the fifty yards separating them, and the dark night, Lily could feel his shock.

"You did that on purpose," she said to Keith.

His gaze cut to hers. "I'm thinking, someday, you'll thank me."

Lily whipped her gaze back to Jared. He looked at her, then turned away and went back into the woods.

UP UNTIL that moment when Jared had seen Keith kissing Lily, he'd found the act of dragging fallen logs and branches through the woods incredibly cathartic. Better than sitting on a bike in a gym. Much better than running laps at the high-school track.

Maybe not quite as good as a marathon bout of up-against-the-wall sex, but then again, he couldn't even remember the last time he'd had that, so he might be remembering it better than it really was.

But he doubted it.

And then he'd gotten that one-two sucker punch to the gut at the sight of Keith with his mouth on Lily.

Damn, that had hurt.

He dumped a whole armful of logs near the fire, and Jack, sitting on top of one of his own previous hauls, held up a hand. "Whoa. We've got more than enough."

"Yeah." Jared kicked a particularly large log, and felt the pain sing up from his toe to his shin. *"Shit."*

"Yeah, the trick is not to let them get to you, dude."

"The wood?"

"Women."

Jared slouched against a tree. "How did you know?"

"It's all over your face." Jack twisted to where he could see Lily still talking to Keith. "Can't blame you either. She's hot."

At Jared's long look, Jack lifted his hands. "Hey, just because I'm hitched, doesn't mean I can't appreciate a good look now and then. But listen, when it comes to women, you've got to take a big mental step back or they'll get you in the heart every single time."

"Yeah? How do you take a step back?"

"You keep yourself just a little removed, you know? I mean, sleep with 'em. Marry 'em if you have to. Just don't hand over your heart on a silver platter."

"So you never gave Michelle your heart?"

"Hell, no. She'd have killed me a long time ago."

Jared watched Lily say something to Keith that made his smile fade.

Good.

Then Keith shook his head, said something else, and Lily touched his cheek and walked away.

Jared liked the look of that even better.

Keith walked away, too, and the knot in Jared's insides loosened slightly so that he could let out a deep breath. He hadn't felt so tense since…since he'd been sitting in the hospital staring in shock at the doctor whose mouth was forming the word *cancer.*

Crazy. Crazy that he felt so strong so soon.

Lily, at her tent, turned, and unerringly, across all the

yards that separated them, found and locked her gaze on Jared's.

Neither of them moved for a long beat, and then finally she crawled into her tent, which she firmly zipped closed.

Jack let out a breath. "Some tension there, huh?"

"Yeah."

Lily's tent shook a little as she moved around in there. Jared pictured her stripping down for bed—an image not helped by the fact he'd had his hands on her now, and wanted them on her again. "You know," he said to Jack. "I think there might be something to opening up and letting a woman in. Really in."

"Sure," Jack explained. "It's called certain death."

"Not every time."

"Ninety-nine-point-nine percent of the time, then."

Jared shook his head, still looking at Lily's tent. It'd gone still. What was she doing now? "Might be worth the risk." He had to think it was. He hadn't been to hell and back to live life the way he'd used to. There had to be more than that, he believed it with every single ounce of heart and soul he had. "Because when you get it right, there's nothing like it."

"Yeah?" Jack looked at him curiously. "And has it ever been right for you?"

"Not yet."

"I rest my case."

"I'm not giving up."

Jack shook his head. "You're in for a world of pain, dude. Seriously."

"It's worth the risk."

"How do you know?"

"Because without it, why bother at all?"

Jack cocked his head to the side as he absorbed that, looking thoughtful now, instead of all-knowing. "To avoid the pain?"

"But one of these days, when it's right, there won't be pain. And then you'll have it all." Jared shrugged. "I just think it's worth the try, that's all."

"Huh." Jack looked at the tent he shared with Michelle. "Yeah, maybe." Standing, he brushed off his hands. "See you in the morning."

Jared watched him vanish into his tent and wished he had the right to be heading toward Lily's with that same intent and purpose. Instead, he headed toward his own. Always, he'd been fine with only himself for company, but now, tonight, as he looked at his empty sleeping bag, he felt lonely.

The hell with this. The hell with not having the right, or being polite and letting her mull things over. The hell with being lonely.

The hell with all of it, and he stepped back out of his tent. The campfire was out, everyone was inside their tents. In the dark night, he headed directly for Lily's. Lightly, he tapped on the canvas door. "Lily?"

No answer.

Hunkering down, he tugged open the zipper enough to stick his head in. "Lily, I—"

But the words caught in his throat, because the tent was empty. He checked the water's edge, checked the entire clearing, and a little bit into the woods.

Nothing.

Then he looked across the lake and saw a movement. She was sitting on the edge of the water, hugging her knees, staring up at the sky.

It took him a while to figure out how to get to her, but he found the trail that led around and came up behind her.

But before he could speak, she stood up and faced him. "Look, here's the thing. I...don't know what I'm doing."

"Lily."

"I'm serious. I don't."

"You seem like you know. You're an incredible guide, Lily."

"I meant with you. I...don't know what I'm doing when it comes to you."

"Well that's okay. We can wing it."

"I came here to find myself. Pre-mistake Lily. Pre-weak Lily. But the thing is, I'm beginning to see I'm never going to live up to that person. I'm not the same anymore. I'm not strong, and there's so much I can't do."

"You're being a little harsh on yourself."

"Just being real."

"So...what, you think that's going to scare me off? Knowing you have doubts and fears like the rest of us humans? I know who you are, Lily, and who you aren't. Now give yourself a moment, you just had an epiphany."

"I'm okay," she whispered. "I don't need—"

"I know." But he pulled her close anyway, and to his surprise, she wrapped her arms around him.

"You see me," she whispered. "You, Jared, the city guy, the business guy, the sophisticated, elegant digital wizard...who'd have thought you could see me?"

He smiled against her hair and held on. Once all of those things, and maybe a small part of him still was.

"But you're also more," she whispered, and if she hadn't worked her way into his heart yet, she did in that very second for understanding him. "So much more, Jared."

He let his mouth brush her temple, then lower, just beneath her ear, and in response, she let out a long shuddery sigh that went through him like an erotic touch. "You're so much more, too, Lily."

She paused at that, as if unfamiliar with the concept. Gliding his hands into her hair, he tugged her head back so that he could get a good look at her mouth, which he wanted on his. "And here's another thought."

"You're going to kiss me?"

"Oh yeah, but first I want you to know something."

Her eyes went wary. "What?"

He put his finger to her silky soft lips. "I think you're the most amazing woman I've ever met."

Her soft exhale warmed his finger, and when she finally smiled, it also warmed his heart. "You're also a little bit stubborn," he added, "in case no one's ever mentioned."

"Uh-huh." Her smile hit her eyes. "Tell me something I don't know."

"How about that you're sexy as hell?"

She stared at him for a long moment. "I need a moment away from here, where I'm not in charge, where I don't have to think. Do you think you can manage any of that?"

She trusted him to take over, to lead, even if only for a little while. "I'm certain I can."

10

LILY FELT Jared's hand slip into hers, and she followed when he gently tugged. In the far recesses of her logical mind, she knew she should send him off to his own tent, and find her way to hers.

She also knew the folly of letting him lead her anywhere in these mountains that he didn't know like she did. But she didn't stop him. Nor, for the first time in her life, did she even attempt to navigate the situation.

She simply let him lead. Wanted him to, so she could shut herself off, just for a little while. It'd been a long, long time since she could do so, certainly since before her accident, and ever since then she'd been fighting that all-consuming, unrelenting fear that she'd never be the same, that she'd not be able to support herself, and any of a myriad of other anxieties and concerns.

She wanted oblivion...nirvana.

Mindlessness.

Jared's broad shoulders blocked out of most of the view of where they headed, and that was fine, that was perfect. For the first time in too long, she emptied her brain of thought, leaving only...emotions.

She'd had only herself to rely on. Or at least that's what she'd always wanted. But somehow, on this trip, that was just another misconception she was discovering.

Leaning on someone might be good. If only for a few...

Jared stepped into the shadows and became a tall, dark sinewy outline of a man. "Come here."

She shifted toward him, and he pulled her down to a rock. She saw they were on the far side of the lake. They were still within earshot of the others, but just out of view.

Fog hovered on the water, drifting over them, smudging the night scenery like a glorious wet painting. With a sigh, Lily let it all surround her, the crickets singing, the branches brushing together in the light breeze.

Her own heartbeat.

Jared didn't say a word, just sat next to her, taking in the magnificent night in utter silence. She looked at him, at his profile with his strong, masculine features and the mouth that she, quite shockingly, wanted on hers. "Jared."

"I want to strip you out of your clothes and take you right here."

"The others—"

"Can hear, I know. We'd be quiet."

The sharp desire in his voice when contrasted to his easy posture, tugged a short laugh out of her. "Uh—"

He looked at her then, his glasses slipping just a little, a frown on his mouth. His stubble had filled in a little after two full days, and his hair had been finger-combed again. Overall impression:

Badass.

When had that happened? Looking at him, a little frisson of sheer desire zinged through her, beginning at her toes, traveling through every single erogenous zone she had, plus a few she'd forgotten about… Yeah, she'd definitely found her oblivion, her nirvana. "Jared."

"I know it sounds crazy," he said. "You could have—"

"Jared."

"—any guy on the planet—"

Cupping his face, she gave him a little shake. *"Jared."*

"Yeah?"

"I don't want to talk," she whispered.

"You don't—"

She kissed him. He didn't protest, and neither did the night. A breeze blew her hair across her face and she impatiently shoved it aside, shooting closer.

With a groan, he pulled her in. She sank into him, the scent of his skin better than any scent she could remember. Around them, the water hit the rocky shore with a rhythmic, almost hypnotic regularity, in tune to their heavy breathing as she strained to get even closer.

She could hear the murmurs of voices—Michelle's and Jack's, she thought. Or maybe Rose's and Rock's. There was something incredibly arousing about that, knowing they were within earshot, especially given what she wanted to do.

"Lily—"

"No. No talking." To that end, she took his mouth again, dancing her tongue to his, absorbing his low groan of pleasure, loving how his arms tightened on her as he kissed her back, hot and deep.

"God, you taste so good," he murmured, dragging kisses along her jaw to her ear. "So damned sweet. I can't get enough."

She couldn't either. His kisses, his touches, were as quietly demanding as the man himself could be. He kissed her again and again, and leaning over her, urged her back on the rock, stretching her out, supporting himself with his hands on either side of her face.

Oh, yeah, now this was what she'd wanted. Desire. Hunger. *More, please.*

Lifting his head, he looked down at her sprawled out beneath him. "You look sweet, too."

She let out a sound that was half laugh, half groan. He needed to shut up and kiss her some more.

"What, no one's ever told you that before?"

"Not exactly."

"Well they should have because you are. And hot. Did I mention you're also hot? So damned hot. Lily—"

"No talking."

"Can't help myself."

"Try harder."

"Maybe if my mouth was busy—" In the interest of her wishes, he kissed the spot beneath her ear, then slowly exhaled, making her shiver wildly.

Good start.

"Mmm." He shifted to her neck, dragging hot, wet open-mouthed kisses down the base of her throat, where she was certain her pulse had approached heart-attack speed.

"And you taste pretty damn hot, too," he said with a

smile, the one that seemed to melt her brain cells and her bones at the same time. "Sweet *and* hot."

The night added to the intimacy. Around her she could hear the things that had always lulled her, soothed her; the crickets, a distant howl…her favorite sounds.

But now she had a new favorite sound—the quickening of Jared's breath as he stared at her hungrily, and also with just a little of a befuddled surprise, as if he couldn't quite believe his luck. Then he bent over her again, touching his mouth to hers, and she knew she'd been right. There was no better way to beat back the emptiness that had taken over than with this. *Him.* Sliding her hands into his short, silky hair, she held him to her.

"Lily—"

"Shh." Beneath him, her body was coming alive, the loneliness and emptiness she'd felt only a short time before with Keith quickly being replaced by a heat that was working outward from everywhere Jared's mouth touched. Then his warm hands slid beneath her T-shirt, skimming over her ribs, his fingertips just barely stroking the undersides of her breasts. Her nipples had long ago hardened, but they hardened further, into two tight, aching peaks.

"I could kiss you all night," he whispered. "Tell me you feel the same."

"Jared Skye, what does *shh* mean? No talking, that's what!" With a huff of impatience, she sat up, pulled off her shirt and tossed it aside. There. She looked up at him, figuring that would finally get her message across.

His gaze took in her white lace bra, his eyes on fire. Rising up to his knees, he pulled off his shirt, too.

Finally. In reward, she ran her hands down his torso, but he backed away.

Huh?

Smiling, he stood up, then kicked off his shoes.

Okay, she liked where this was going. A lot.

And then he shucked his pants. Yeah, she really liked where this was going…

There he was standing beneath the meager starlight naked as the day he was born.

She licked her suddenly dry lips. "Okay, that works. Now—"

But she was talking to herself because he'd turned, and without a single word—which was just as she'd asked so what could she say?—he dived into the water in one clean, cat-like movement.

Sitting up, she stared in disbelief at the black ripples on the lake until he re-emerged and tossed the water from his wet hair.

Without a moon for light, she couldn't be sure, but she thought maybe he was grinning.

"Come on," he said, and lifted a hand.

"Skinny-dipping?"

"Why not?"

"Because…" *Because I'd thought you'd be inside me by now.* "It's juvenile."

"Actually…" He stood up so that the water lapped at his shins. His body gleamed by the meager starlight as water sluiced off him, down his shoulders, his arms, his chest, his belly…

Lower, and, oh yes, she looked. He was aroused, hugely so, and her mouth went dry. God, he was a beautiful man, so beautiful she wanted to lap him up one sip at a time.

"I don't feel so juvenile," he said very silkily.

Oh boy.

"You coming in?"

"I don't know," she murmured, still staring at him. She'd wanted mindless, wild, animal sex. Him inside, her wild, no thoughts allowed.

And yet everything he did, every time he touched her, or spoke, or even just looked at her, her thoughts raced. She was yearning and burning, all of her, *not* just her body but her heart and soul, and that scared her deep.

Damn it, she'd just wanted to have some mutually satisfying sex, that's all. Why couldn't he oblige?

As if reading her mind, he let out a slow, daring smile. "What's wrong? Someone else took charge of the moment, and you lost your place?"

She opened her mouth. Then carefully closed it again. "No."

But he laughed. "Yeah."

"You're pissing me off."

"I know it." He splashed her, just scooped his hand into the water and splashed her, wetting her from her roots to her toes and all the places in between, including her bra. Water dripped off her nose as she looked at him. "That was juvenile, as well."

"Yeah? What are you going to do about it?"

"I'm sitting here without my shirt on, and you want to play?"

"Uh-huh."

"You're crazy." But she toed off her shoes.

He smiled.

"I don't want any strings between us," she said, pointing at him. "Just this." She unzipped her jeans. "Got it?"

"This being…"

"Us. Naked." She unhooked her bra. "Can you handle that?"

He was still smiling. "What if you decide you want more?"

"I won't." She let her bra fall. *"Can you handle it?"* she asked again.

"I can sure as hell try."

And then she slid her jeans and panties down in one fell swoop. His smile faltered, replaced by a fiery look of desire that stole her breath.

"Come here," he said very softly, and held out his hand.

A light breeze blew over her and she shivered as she stepped into the water, reaching out for him. He pulled her in, tight, close, and just like that, at the feel of his wet, warm body against hers, he banished the chill.

He kissed her as he pulled them both down into the water, and as the water closed around their shoulders, lapping at their bodies, she tasted the inside of his mouth and found unbelievable comfort in the familiarity of him.

Comfort, even as she wanted him to make her explode. So, *so* unbelievable. But at least she wasn't alone in this odd phenomenon. She could hear his ragged breathing, as well, feel the pounding of his heart as he nudged her even closer, wrapping one arm around her lower back, the other sliding into her hair to tug her face up to his. He felt it, too, whatever "it" was, and a little stunned, a little overwhelmed at it all, she touched his jaw.

"Lily," he whispered, his longing making his voice thick and husky.

She was a strong swimmer, and yet he held her up in the water. It felt incredible, leaning on him, letting him do the work, knowing he wouldn't let go. Her toes bumped his shins, their bare thighs slid together. His hard abs pressed into her softer ones, and without conscious thought she ran her hands up his chest and around his neck, pressing her mouth to his for more of his achingly slow, melting kisses.

She hoped like hell no one else decided to go for a late-night naked swim, but then he slid a hand down her spine, stopping to squeeze her butt before stroking further, down the back of her leg, urging it around his waist, which opened her up for him, and oh God, he arched his hips into hers so that she could feel exactly what she did to him.

He was hard, gloriously so, and boldly nudging at her opening, and she forgot all about the others.

He was a stranger, and yet she'd never felt closer to anyone in her life. Pressed even closer, she made a sound of intense need, and he met her more than halfway, his mouth welcoming hers, harder and deeper this time, as if he'd pulled the plug on any hesitancy, on the leash of his control. His hands roamed wildly over her, and hers did the same, and when she wrapped her fingers around his glorious erection, he swore and staggered unsteadily, and they both fell.

Water closed over their heads, and laughing breathlessly, they crawled to the shore. Lily lay back on the sand, her head and torso out of the water, looking up at Jared as he towered over her, his eyes glittering.

"God, you're beautiful," he whispered, lowering his body to hers as the water lapped at their calves. "So damned beautiful you take my breath." He buried his face in her hair, then her neck, breathing her in as if he meant to inhale her, his hands skimming up and down her body, spreading the heat within her.

When she opened her legs for him, he groaned, low and raw, and made himself at home between them, cupping her face for another soul-wrenching kiss. Then he took that kiss on a cruise down her throat to her breasts, and she couldn't help it, she cried out.

"Shh," he murmured, and sucked her hard into his mouth.

It turned out it was hard to "shh." She tried, she really did, she just couldn't, so he put his fingers over her lips and slid further down her body, kissing each rib, her belly button.

Lower.

Oh. God.

Slipping his hands beneath her, he lifted her high enough that he could kiss her.

There.

And with the water lapping at her legs and Jared lapping at her center, he took her right out of herself and back again, leaving her gripping wet sand in her fists, staring blindly up at the stars, shuddering, stunned.

"Again," he commanded, and though she'd just exploded so hard she thought she couldn't come again, he proved her wrong.

Twice.

Good lord. He might have been a classic workaholic, a self-described ordinary working stiff, but there was nothing ordinary about what he did to her there on the shore. Whatever his experience had or hadn't been, he was earthy, giving, a masterful lover, and even when she had him in her hands, making him tremble and swear as she slowly stroked, he took care of her, almost intuitively knowing what she needed and when, which was him, inside her.

When he sank into her, their twin groans mingled in the night air, and when he began to move, she couldn't have come up with her own name.

"Lily."

Right. Her name was Lily. Good. Great. But she promptly forgot it again because he'd opened his eyes and locked them on hers, letting her see what she did to him, letting her watch the pleasure, the hunger, the sheer need for her roll over him, through him, and back into her.

No one had ever been this deep within her before, inside her body, her mind, her soul.

No one.

And she gave herself up to it. Really, she had no choice. It was the first true joy she'd experienced in a very long time. Given the look in his eyes, he felt the same. Marveling, she touched his jaw, his mouth, her heart quickening as he kissed her fingers and thrust deep within her.

Unbelievably, she felt her body tightening again, but then he did the one thing she wanted him to never do— he stopped.

"Lily—"

"No. Please don't stop." Was that her, all breathless and panty, sounding like Marilyn Monroe? Yeah, and she didn't care, all pride had deserted her, because damn it, she needed him to keep moving, she needed that more than she needed anything else in the entire world. Her toes were curling, her body on the very edge. "Please, please…"

"God." Dropping his forehead to hers, he panted for breath. "Lily, don't move."

"I have to." Arching up, she wrapped her legs around his waist, which brought him even deeper within her, and they both gasped in pure, unadulterated pleasure. "Jared, you have to—"

"No condom." He grated this out, his fingers gripping her hips as if she was his lifeline.

Condom.

How she'd nearly put that little thought right out of her head was beyond her, but he'd fried her brain cells. "Front pocket of my jeans."

He blinked. "You have a condom in your pocket?"

She stared up at him. "I think the correct reaction here is gratitude."

"Oh, trust me." He reached up for the clothes they'd tossed on the shore, and fumbled through her pocket. "It is sheer gratitude. I'm also flattered." He was back, kneeling between her thighs, his hands sliding slowly up her legs, his gaze following his own movements, his breathing going ragged again.

"Hurry," she panted.

"On it." But he leaned in and kissed her inner thigh, then turning his head, nuzzled her very center.

Her gasp filled the quiet night. Lifting his head, his eyes were dark as he tore open the packet and rolled the condom down his length. Then he was poised at her opening, going still as he looked at her. "So beautiful," he murmured.

She touched his mouth, his jaw, then sank her fingers into his hair to tug him closer. "Kiss me," she whispered, rocking up to meet him, and when he sank into her again, she let out a sound of sheer relief. Between the dark night, the heat between their bodies, and the power of his thrusts, she was lost. *Lost.*

And apparently he felt the same way, because he tore his mouth from hers and arched his back to thrust even deeper, gripping her hips as he did, his gaze locked on hers, driving her higher and higher, watching her with eyes gone glossy with passion. He was beautiful, too, so beautiful, and then, with a surprised cry, she shattered again, and this time, took him with her.

It took a good long moment to come back to herself, and when she did, the night air was cooling her damp skin, blowing her hair in her flushed face as she lay bare-ass naked on a rock with an equally bare-ass naked man she'd known all of a few days holding her tight to him.

Oh, boy.

Sitting up, she reached for her top.

Beside her, Jared sighed. "Fun time over?"

She'd told him she didn't want any strings, just this. She'd made sure he knew that, and yet she'd forgotten one tiny little thing—to believe it herself. Now she was fighting the urge to cling, and that was just disconcerting enough to have her needing to run for cover. "I should get back." Yeah, that was it.

He watched as she slipped into her jeans and shoved her panties in her pocket. She pushed her hair out of her face and looked for her ponytail holder, but it'd vanished. Willing to write it off, she jammed her feet into her shoes.

"What was it," he asked quietly as he rose. "The intimacy? Or the fact that you engaged your heart?"

Her entire body went from limp-as-a-noodle satisfied to drawn tight as a bow. "Not that I have to explain myself here, but I prefer not to lie around naked for anyone else to find us."

"No one is even going to look for us." He smiled grimly. "It was both. We got too close too soon, and you regret it."

"I don't do regret."

"Right. You just shut yourself off."

She turned to face him as he pulled up his jeans. "Shut myself off?"

"Sure." He jammed an arm into his shirt. "That's easier than facing the truth, right?"

"And what is the truth?" she asked, knowing she wasn't going to like this one little bit.

He buttoned his shirt atop the abs she'd just had her hands all over. "That what we did got a little too close for comfort. And now you need to back off. You need to be alone, where you can tell yourself that no, you didn't just nearly come right outside yourself because it was *that* amazing."

She put her hands on her hips and absorbed that unexpected punch of truth. "A little sure of yourself, aren't you?"

"No." He laughed harshly. "Hell, no. It's just that I was there, Lily, and I know damn well that's not how it usually is. At least for me." He shoved his fingers through his hair and just looked at her.

She knew what he wanted to hear. That no, hell no, it wasn't usually like that for her either, but she was still reeling from what he'd pulled out of her. She was nearly staggering with it.

This was so *not* what she'd expected tonight.

She'd wanted a little escape, a little fun, a little oblivion, that's all. Only what she'd found was so much more than that.

So much more.

Hating that he was right, about everything, she turned away and started back toward camp. "Actually, my usual MO is just to walk away," she called back. *Like she was doing right now, as a matter of fact.* "'Night, Jared."

"*Lily.*"

She turned back and lifted her chin. "I warned you."

"That this would be just sex." He stood there watching her, hair standing straight up, eyes sleepy and sexy, clothes rumpled. Rumpled. "Yes, yes you did warn me, thank you. Your conscience can be clear."

"I hope this won't affect our working relationship."

He just looked at her in disbelief, and yeah, she felt stupid. *Working relationship?* God. "Good night," she managed around a thick throat, knowing she was being impossibly rude, but was utterly unable to stop herself.

She'd been looking for herself, and here she was. Pathetic. Weak. Needy.

And she'd let him see.

"If we don't talk about it," he warned as she turned away again. "You're going to dream about it. About me."

Yeah, of that, she had no doubt.

_11_

OF COURSE she dreamed of him, how could she not? What Jared had done to her in the woods by the lake's edge beneath a starlit sky, had been the most erotic, sensual time of her life, and she wasn't likely to forget it.

She'd wanted oblivion and he'd delivered. In spades. She stared at the ceiling of her tent, her body _still_ humming with the aftermath of great sex.

It'd been a while, she told herself. That's why she'd gone off like that.

But now she had to face the dreaded morning after. No regrets, she reminded herself, and, facing the music, got up, dressed, and left her tent. Keith was gone, which was vintage Keith.

She'd turned him down, however gently, and he'd moved on without a backwards glance.

Just as he had the first time.

She looked around at the group of tents, at the fire she'd rekindled, and felt a real pang. She did love doing this. She had, for a few days at least, loved the thought of continuing to do it, even though it'd meant roots, ties.

Relationships.

Hadn't it happened already, with Jared? At that thought, another not-so-little pang tugged at her heart, which only proved her point. If the thought of walking away from him was hurting already, she was in far too deep.

Rubbing the ache in her lower back, she got to work. No looking back, she told herself firmly. She'd done too much of that and it hadn't gotten her anywhere but Heartache City.

From now on, forward was the only direction she'd move in. Over-Herself City, here she came.

ROSE WOKE UP early for the third time ever and rewarded herself with a bath in the lake, which turned out to be cold enough to shock her skin into glowing like a twenty-year-old's. Go figure, she'd just given herself a cheap spa day. Laughing at herself, she put on her makeup and headed back to camp.

Lily was cooking breakfast, which made her a hero in Rose's book. She was also pretending not to be watching Jared's tent for signs of life, something she understood extremely well because she'd made a new Olympic event out of watching Rock the Cutie Patootie. "Smells delish," she said with a smile.

"It is delish," Lily responded, and handed her a plate. "But I'm afraid you've wasted your mascara. You know we're going canoeing today."

Rose took a peek at Rock's tent and was relieved to see him coming out of the woods with his toothbrush. He wore his black jeans, black boots and a black T-shirt that emphasized the physique that made her need a bib.

Good Lord, the boy was hot. "It's waterproof, and don't worry, a good application of makeup is never wasted. God, he's such a muffin. I just want to spread him with butter and eat him up. Do you think I'm getting anywhere with him at all?"

Rock looked over at the two of them and smiled.

Lily waved and began the next omelet as she answered. "And where is it you want to be getting?"

"Preferably in his pants."

Lily nearly dropped her pan, making Rose laugh. "Come on, I am not shocking you."

"No. No, you're not, but jeez, Rose, at least wait until I eat something."

"Like *you* don't want to get into someone's pants."

Lily kept her eyes on the pan. "Not before breakfast I don't."

"You're not fooling anyone, you know." Rose gestured with her chin over Lily's shoulder to where Jared appeared from his tent; six feet of long-legged, leanly muscled, rumpled man.

With eyes for no one else, he looked right at Lily, and Rose let out a low whistle. "Hold on tight, Lily, it's going to be a bumpy ride."

Lily burned her finger. "Damn it."

Rose laughed softly. "So you've already been there, done that then?"

"Rose."

"Come on, admit it. The sexual tension between the two of you is enough to ignite the treetops."

"That's ridiculous."

"So you deny wanting him?"

Lily turned away, but her bright-red neck gave her away. "I've got to get cooking," she said.

Rose laughed. "Honey, you know you already are."

YEAH, SHE WAS COOKING. Lily stole another peek at Jared. His lightweight cargos were neat and clean—how the hell did he do that?—his T-shirt wrinkle-free. She knew the outdoor gear was alien to the man who'd lived in an office for so many years, and yet he wore it as if he'd been born outside.

He had something in his back pocket, something she'd bet money was digital, which would normally annoy her, but with him, it somehow made her sigh because it meant there was indeed a rebel in him.

And God, she was such a sucker for a rebel.

He was helping Michelle and Jack take down their tent, and laughing at something Michelle said.

The sound of his amusement drifted over her, into her. In the past year he'd been to hell and back, and yet he looked so carefree, easygoing.

He hadn't always been that way, she knew that, he'd told her. People changed, and she knew that, too.

Did she want to change?

She was stubborn, set in her ways. A bit of a handful. How many times had she heard that? Her lifestyle didn't exactly bode well for a relationship of any kind, and hell, she didn't even know if *he* was interested in a relationship, but...but if he was...could she?

Would she?

God. It was a cool morning, complete with a chilly breeze, and she was sweating. "It's hot already, huh?"

Rose laughed. "Baby, that's all man making you hot. Admit it."

"Rose."

"Admit. It."

Lily laughed. What else could she do? And Rose laughed with her, giving her a one-armed hug while still holding onto her plate. "Ah, look at that. You're so pretty when you smile. You ought to try it more often."

When Rose walked away, Lily stared into the fire. Didn't she smile all the time? Okay, maybe not.

At least, not until the past few days anyway, because she felt as if lately she'd been smiling non-stop, at least when one certain man looked at her.

"Hey."

Speaking of said man. He was standing right behind her, and she didn't need to look down at her suddenly happy nipples to know that her body recognized him without even turning around.

When she didn't respond, he merely turned her to face him. Nope, no avoiding the whole morning-after thing, not with this guy. He was too direct for that.

"You okay?" he asked.

"Fine and dandy. You?"

His mouth quirked. "Fine and dandy."

"Good, because we're going canoeing. You'll need every ounce of energy you have."

"I'm up for it. Lily—"

She thrust a plate in his hands. "Eat."

"About last n—"

"You really need to eat, because it's a big day. We're going to start at the northeastern tip of the Balsam Rim and end up at its southwestern reach. Hard work, but for a reward, we'll spend the night on a precipice among giant spruce and Fraser firs. It's unforgettable."

"Lily—"

"Oh, and we'll walk through a forest that only just barely escaped the saw during the area's former life as timber-company land. It's a gotta-see, so yeah, get eating. Grab some bacon." She jerked her chin towards the tray, avoiding his hazel eyes. "There's melon, as well. Do you like melon?"

"Melon?" he asked doubtfully. "We're going to talk about melon?"

"Well, we could go back to the whole timberland thing."

He just looked at her.

"Fine," she said on a long suffering sigh. "What else would we talk about?" Most men would go running now, she thought grimly. Yep, any second he'd do just that.

But he didn't go anywhere. "Gee, I don't know," he said dryly. "How about how much energy we used up last night, and how good it felt? No, make that amazing." He stepped close, let her see the heat in his eyes. "It felt amazing, Lily."

She broke eye contact to study the fire. "I'd rather discuss food."

"Okay, you go ahead and do that. I can wait you out."

"Jared." She closed her eyes. "We can't do this now. I've got breakfast to serve. And then the canoe guy to meet on the river, and…"

And she couldn't handle talking about last night.

She just couldn't. She took a deep breath, held it, then slowly let it out. "And I don't think talking about it is going to help."

Silence from Jared.

"We're both adults," she said, filling it. "And what happened between us here in the mountains—"

"Should stay in the mountains?"

Her eyes flew open. Jared was gone.

In his place was Jack, who'd clearly moved in close while she'd been talking to herself, and was looking pretty amused.

Jared now stood on the far side of the fire, holding his plate, chewing on a piece of bacon, watching the flames.

"Damn it," she said, and ignoring Jack's soft laugh at her side, she began another omelet.

"Hey, *someone* should be getting some out here," Jack said. "I've always wanted to make it in the wilds. Tell me, do you get mosquito bites in private places when you strip down, because—"

"Jack?" she said sweetly.

He shoved a bite into his mouth. "Yes?"

"Shut up and eat." She refilled his plate with more bacon and tried to pretend she wasn't blushing.

She also refused to look at him again, or at Jared for that matter, and spent the next half hour cleaning up. Then she made sure that Michelle ate so that she wouldn't be able to complain about hunger a half hour down the river, that Rose didn't eat Rock for her nourishment, that everyone was happy and content and ready to go.

Because she was—at least the ready to go part. The happy and content? Not so much.

WATER LAPPED at Lily's canoe, which she was sharing with Jack at the moment. In front of her, Rose and Michelle, who'd not wanted to be with Jack because she wanted to sun instead of paddle. Ahead of them were Jared and Rock.

Everyone was doing well, though her gaze kept straying to Jared. There was nothing more relaxing or soul-rewarding than canoeing down a slow-moving river—that is if she could take her mind off things.

Hope this won't affect our working relationship. Had she really said that? Yes. Yes, she had, and she winced at the stupidity of it all over again.

Of course it was going to affect their working relationship. He'd watched her strip naked for him. He'd had his hands on every inch of her.

And his mouth. God, his mouth. He'd had that on every inch of her, as well, and she was pretty sure she'd screamed his name.

Several times.

Feeling her face heat, she groaned and shook her head, trying to dispel the image.

But it stuck. It all stuck—Jared dropping his clothes and driving into the water, then getting her to do the same. And then...and then showing her how to relax and lose herself with a mutually satisfying sweaty bout of sex.

Okay, more than just sex.

Damn it.

"You okay?"

She looked at Jack. "Um, yeah. Fine."

This was all Jared's fault. Last night, he'd stood there with the water lapping at his feet, looking so decidedly un-city-like, and incredibly gorgeous. The way he'd crawled up her body as she lay sprawled over the rock. How he'd spread her legs with his, then taken a good long look at her. Then he'd done a lot more than just look...

Now, in the river, paddling away to get out some aggression, she felt her nipples harden beneath her life-vest. Yeah, *that* was professional.

But it was nothing compared to what was going on between her thighs.

Or beneath her ribs, damn it, in the region of her heart. Now *that* reaction, *that* was the scary part.

Jack was looking at her again, and she forced a smile. *Still fine.*

As she thought it, Jared slowed his and Rock's canoe until it came even with theirs. Jared was wielding a paddle as if he'd been born to it, and he gave her a look that for once she couldn't read.

He didn't say anything.

She didn't either.

After a moment of the silent stand-off, his mouth quirked, though the smile didn't quite reach his eyes.

And then he paddled on.

"Whew," Jack said quietly. "Is it me, or is it getting hot out here?"

"Funny." She watched Jared go, her chest tightening. She'd told him she didn't do regrets, so she had no business going there in her head. It didn't matter how he'd looked as she'd walked away from him, his hair rumpled, his eyes dark and sexy, his body loose and still damp...

God. Her knees actually wobbled whenever she

thought about it, so really, it was a good thing they were canoeing on the river today instead of hiking.

She forced herself to look around her at the tall, majestic mountains, at the utter serenity all around them, and came to an understanding with herself.

She truly did love it out here. She loved what she was doing, loved having people with her to share it with, loved all of it.

And weak or strong, she was meant to be here.

A laugh behind her brought her out of herself, and she whipped around in time to watch Rose flash Rock her bare breasts. She was standing to do so, her top up over her face.

"Rose," Rock said quickly, clearly torn between looking at the admittedly spectacular breasts and the now unsteady canoe. "Your canoe—"

"Uh-oh," Rose gasped, because her motions had caused the canoe to rock back and forth, higher each time.

In the same unsteady canoe, Michelle screamed.

So did Rose. "Ohmigod—"

"Rose!" Lily called out. "Don't make any quick moves, just—"

Rose sat, grabbing onto the sides of the canoe for dear life.

Too little too late. Especially when combined with Michelle's own frantic movements. The canoe rocked even more. Rose was still screaming as the canoe rocked, rocked, rocked…right over, and settled, upside down.

As Rose and Michelle hit the water in tandem, the screaming abruptly stopped.

"Michelle!" Jack yelled, grabbing the sides of his and Lily's canoe as he stood, clearly freaking out. *"Michelle!"*

Uh-oh. They began rocking, too, violently. "Jack, sit!" Lily yelled. *Jesus, did no one listen?* "You've got to—"

Too late. Their canoe rolled over, too, and she and Jack joined Michelle in the brink.

Damn it. Once again cold water closed over her head. She broke the surface and shoved her hair out of her eyes. Jared paddled up next to her and offered her the tip of his paddle to hold on to. "You all right?"

She looked into his eyes and had to shake her head. "Saving me again?"

He smiled. "If I am, does that mean you'll owe me?"

"Ha-ha." She struggled to flip the canoes, and Jared slipped into the water to help her. "Thanks," she said, and at his easy smile, she sighed. "Fine. I really do owe you."

"Aren't you going to ask me what I want?"

She shrugged. "I can figure it out."

He actually looked insulted at that. "Well, since you're so sure," he murmured, and then, pulling his and Rock's canoe free, he paddled away, leaving her to wonder as she watched them go…had she misjudged him by accident, or on purpose so as to further alienate him?

Neither said anything flattering about herself, that was certain.

_12_

BY THE TIME they stopped for a picnic lunch, Jack was starving. He'd worked up an appetite while watching his wife bounce around in her wet bikini the past few hours.

Rose's bikini wasn't bad either. She sat in the grass clearing eating her sandwich, shrugging off her earlier adventure. "Just a waste of a good hair day, that's all."

Michelle, however, hadn't quite found her happy place yet, not that Jack was surprised. The woman had the corner on grudge-holding. "This is so not a vacation," she said to no one in particular. "Cooking without a kitchen, putting up tents before you can go to sleep, carting everything around that you need—"

"Really?" Jack interjected. "All that cooking, and putting up your own tent is getting to you, huh?"

She sighed. "You know what I mean. You're not used to this either. You're much more at home behind a desk and your computer, where everything you need is online at your fingertips."

"As I recall, the last thing I did online was to put something on one of _your_ fingers," he said, and all eyes slid to the huge diamond glittering on Michelle's ring finger.

It had cost him big, but he'd loved, *loved,* buying it for her. Loved knowing he could. But Michelle lifted a shoulder. "Easy enough to buy something like this with Daddy's money."

Jack stared at her, stung. "Probably. If that's what I'd done."

She blinked, her baby blues confused. "What?"

"My computer consulting business," Jack said evenly. "It's doing well. It'd doing *real* well. I tried to tell you."

"But...Daddy told you to use his account whenever you bought me something."

"Maybe *I* wanted to buy you something. I am your husband, you know. It's allowed."

She looked at him as if he was an alien.

Jack looked back.

Michelle laughed, as if he'd told a joke, but Jack just kept looking at her. "You...bought the ring?"

Jack nodded, and Michelle stared down at the ring as if seeing it for the first time. "Oh."

Jack touched it, and then Michelle surprised him by entangling his fingers in hers, holding on. When he looked into her eyes, she shot him a tentative smile, but it was real. After a moment, he returned it with a slow smile of his own.

Maybe, just maybe, he thought, this trip would pay for itself yet.

Lily handed out cookies, which everyone devoured on the spot. Jack ate his, and half of Michelle's, who tossed back her now dry hair. "Yeah, it's too bad I didn't get hurt today," she said, trying to see herself in Jack's reflective sunglasses. "I could have gotten airlifted right out of here. A first-class ticket back to civilization."

"Just you, huh?" Jack asked.

"Well, you're having such a good time…"

He looked around at everyone, no longer surprised that he was. He was having a ball, thanks to the great company, not to mention the lack of his father-in-law. "Well, yeah, actually. I am."

"But see, you could have a good time anywhere," Michelle said. "In a Dumpster for God's sake."

His stomach knotted all over again, and he set down his drink. "I could, yes. If you were there, too."

Michelle's brow furrowed. "You mean…"

"Yeah."

She looked confused. "That's…"

"Marriage?" he asked softly.

Michelle stared at him, eyes suddenly suspiciously bright. "Yeah," she whispered softly, and warming him as nothing else could have, she ran her fingers over his jaw. "Thanks, Jack. You always have a way of making me feel special. Loved."

"You are," he said, turning his face to kiss her palm.

"Ah, that's so sweet," Rose whispered. She wore one of Rock's sweatshirts, and sighed dreamily as she reached for his hand. "Young love. There's nothing like it."

"Yeah." Michelle sipped at her soda, eyes on Jack. "Nothing like it." And she smiled and leaned in to kiss his cheek.

Jack pulled her onto his lap, hugging her hard, thinking ahead to tonight, when maybe she'd show some more of this whole loving thing.

THEY CANOED until the river spilled into a gorgeous alpine lake surrounded by towering pines and staggeringly tall majestic mountains.

For the second day in a row, Jared looked around at the amazing landscape and felt an increasing tug on his heart. He glanced at Lily, who was making camp in their grassy clearing overlooking the water, helping everyone get settled, and marveled.

She was amazing, too. By turns she took his breath and moved him, and looking at her now, he thought maybe he did the same for her. Or hoped he did.

Earlier, she'd met up with a staff member of Outdoor Adventures for the canoe pickup and new supply drop, after which Lily had served stew, corn bread and salad.

Now Jared brought her wood to stoke the fire. "Keith didn't make the drop this time."

She watched him dump the wood into the pile. "Hey, you don't have to haul wood."

"I like to haul wood." He squatted in front of her and waited until she looked at him. "No Keith?"

"No."

"You okay?"

She looked around her, took a deep breath, and smiled. "Actually...yes."

She said that as if half-afraid it wouldn't last. Then as if karma was proving her right, a scream split the air.

Michelle's.

LILY RAN TOWARD Michelle and Jack's tent. Michelle had pretty much desensitized Lily to the sound of her scream but she still had to investigate.

What now? she wondered. What could it possibly be now?

Loud crying came from inside the tent. "What happened?" Lily asked Jack, then turned to the sobbing tent. *"Michelle?"*

"He br-brought me a present," she hiccupped from inside. "N-not more diamonds."

Jack sighed. "Michelle, I'm sorry. I didn't know you wouldn't like it."

"Like what?" Lily asked him.

He spread his hands helplessly. "I was just trying to bring her something different, you know? Something that didn't have money signs attached to it."

"A frog!" Michelle cried through the tent wall. "He set it right in my hands, and it was *slimy!* It leapt onto my head. *In my hair, Lily!"*

Rock chuckled and Rose glared at him. His smile faded. "That's…awful," he stammered.

"It was figurative," Jack said, sounding desperate, like a man who knew he was going down with his ship. "You know, like a gift from the heart, one that didn't cost a thing."

Rock leaned in. "Dude," he said to Jack. "Next time go with a rock or something."

Jack appealed to all of them. "Look, I just thought that something alive, something breathing, would better symbolize what I was trying to say about our marriage."

From inside the tent, the crying slowed.

"I wanted her to know it matters," he said. "It matters a lot. *She* matters a lot."

"Michelle?" Lily asked, meeting Jack's gaze. "Still with us?"

The crying stopped completely. The rasp of a zipper filled the air, and then Michelle stuck her head out and stared up at Jack. "You weren't trying to freak me out?"

"No!" He looked horrified. "Jeez, I wouldn't do that to you."

Michelle chewed on her lower lip, studying her husband for a long moment.

"Well, I think it was a beautiful gesture," Rock said in his new friend's defense.

Everyone looked at him.

"It was," he insisted. "He wanted to keep their marriage *alive,* get it?"

"Thanks, man," Jack said, but he had eyes only for Michelle. Longing and love and confusion and worry and need all warred for room in his expression, and Lily's heart tugged hard.

Relationships were expensive. They cost blood and sweat and tears, and worse, they hurt.

And yet, looking at Jack working so hard to meet Michelle halfway, while not even fully understanding why she was upset with him, got to her.

What would it be like to have a man love her so much that he would do anything, whatever it took, to be there for her, to win her love?

She had no idea, because she'd never let anyone get that close. It'd been all about self-protection with her, being strong enough to take care of herself, but now she wondered at all she'd missed because of it. Excusing herself under the guise of cleaning up dinner, she went to the lake to wash her pans.

This wasn't about her, she reminded herself. It was about the group she'd brought here, and making their time and money well spent.

This lake was larger than the others they'd seen, and heavily wooded, so much so that from the alcove she was hunkered in, she couldn't see camp.

That worked for her. She picked up a small, round rock and skimmed it across the water. They'd gone twenty miles today on the canoes, but this lake reminded her of last night's, where she'd watched Jared take off his clothes—

"I have an idea," he said softly behind her, and she barely managed not to jump out of her skin. Evening out her features, she turned to face the tall, rangy shadow. He stepped forward, and the moonlight fell over him as he offered her that crooked smile, the one that never failed to turn her heart on its side.

"This time," he said "when you say you don't want to talk, I'll believe you."

She had to laugh. "You really think we're going to have a repeat? That I'm going to just take all my clothes off and dive in?"

"I'm hoping," he said so fervently she laughed again.

But the laughter faded when he pulled off his glasses and stepped close, touching her cheek, whispering her name in a voice of longing and desire. "I've been thinking about this all day."

"What?"

With a smile, he kissed her, achingly gentle, sweet,

and in spite of herself, she slid her fingers into his short hair to hold him to her. But given the sound that rumbled from his throat as he tugged her closer and deepened the kiss, he had no intention of going anywhere. Then he touched his tongue to hers and it was *her* turn to make a low, desperate sound of need as she staggered back a step, coming up against a tree.

"Mmm," he said following her, his mouth fastened on her neck as he sandwiched her between the hard trunk of the tree and the even harder length of his body. "I can't get enough of you."

"I thought you said we didn't have to talk."

He let out a soft huff of laughter against her skin as he spread hot, open-mouthed kisses to her shoulder, scraping aside her loose T-shirt as he went. "I can't help it," he murmured. "I want to eat you up, Lily. All of you."

Before she could say a word to that, he'd dropped to his knees and opened her jeans.

"Jared—"

"Right here," he said, and kissed the wedge of skin he'd exposed, just above her panty line, low on her hip.

"Um—"

His mouth skimmed a little lower, and she lost her train of thought. *"Jared."*

"Yeah, you already said that." One tug and her jeans were at her thighs.

"Yes, but—"

Another tug and her panties followed, leaving her bared to the night and Jared's gaze.

"But..." he coaxed patiently, his breath warming her skin.

Her head thunked back against the tree. "I..."

His hands skimmed her thighs, as if needing to touch as much of her as he could, and then his thumbs scraped down, down...opening her to him.

"Ohmigod," she whispered when he leaned in, unerringly gliding his tongue right where she needed it the most.

"You were trying to say something," he said silkily, and then used his tongue again, in another slow, mind-blowing stroke.

"I...I can't think when you do that." Her hands went to his head, her fingers tightening on his hair as he continued to drive her out of her ever-loving mind. "Wait," she gasped.

He paused, his mouth hovering a fraction of an inch from her quivering flesh. "So you *do* want to talk?"

"No. Yes." She gulped for breath. In truth, she had no idea what she wanted. "God. What are we doing?"

"Having wild monkey sex, I hope."

She had to laugh, though it was shaky. "Here, Jared?"

He let his fingers do the talking, slipping one into her while his thumb slowly stroked.

Her knees wobbled. Again her head hit the tree trunk. "Yeah, okay. Here."

In answer, he pulled her down to the ground.

"HURRY, JARED. Hurry, hurry..."

With a breathless laugh, Jared rolled over on top of Lily, pinning her down as he smoothed the hair from her face. "Impatient woman."

"That's just one of my very fine qualities."

He nudged his hips to hers. "Maybe patience isn't a requirement."

"Good." she murmured this in that throaty, I-need-to-come voice. "I hear patience is overrated anyway."

God, he loved that voice. Jared stared down at her mouth, thinking he loved her mouth, too. Then her lips curved, and he thought of all the things he wanted her to do with them… She lay there, sprawled out for all the crickets and the stars and God to see, looking so gorgeous he could hardly stand it.

He came up on one elbow for the sheer pleasure of getting a better look at her. Oh yeah, perfection. He kissed the tip of her nose, her chin. He kissed her shoulder, and then shoved up her shirt to kiss a breast, taking the time to run his tongue over her nipple, smiling against her skin when she let out a shuddery sigh and mustered up the strength to hold his head in place, as if she didn't want him to lose his train of thought and move away.

Fat chance. He licked her other nipple, then began making his way south, and when he got to ground zero, she gasped and arched up into his mouth.

Perfect.

He held her still for the assault, soaking up the soft, sexy whimpers that left her throat, enjoying very much the tight hold she had on his hair. At this rate, she was going to make him bald, but he'd been there from the chemo and nothing scared him anymore.

Except maybe not being with her.

Yeah, that sounded scary. He'd have to do something about that possibility, but, for now, he planned on taking Lily straight to heaven.

WHEN LILY returned to planet earth, she lay on the ground with Jared sprawled out next to her, head propped up by one hand, the other stroking the length of her.

She felt like a limp noodle, but despite the laziness of his pose, she could feel the tension still within his body. He hadn't asked, he wouldn't, but she knew what *she* wanted to do next.

Coming up on her knees, she smiled down at him.

He'd put his glasses back on. Now he looked up at her, his glasses a little fogged, which made her smile widen.

"What?" he asked.

"You're cute."

"Cute," he repeated, as if unsure this was a good thing.

She removed his glasses. "Very cute."

"Puppy cute?" he asked, squinting up at her. "Or gotta-have-me cute?"

"Both." She unbuttoned his jeans and carefully pulled down his zipper, humming in approval at what she found, which was him, aroused and ready for her.

"Tell me you restocked your pocket supply," he said unsteadily when she bent over him and did as he'd done—took her tongue on a happy tour.

"Mmmhmm," she murmured around a mouthful.

Slipping his fingers into her hair, he tugged her head up so he could see her face. "Please God, say that was a yes," he begged.

"Yes."

Apparently that was all he needed to hear. Rolling them over until he was on top of her, hard between her legs, he reached for her jeans. Specifically, her pocket. Triumphant, he protected them both, then entwining his fingers in hers, brought their joined hands up to either side of her head. Bending to kiss her, he slid home. And then took them both right out of themselves.

It might have been minutes, hours, or even days later when Jared rolled off Lily, gasping for breath.

Lily did the same.

Together they stared up at the night sky, waiting for the air to return to their lungs. Lily could have stayed right there, skin damp, the air cooling them, Jared still panting for air next to her for...well, much longer, but...

Ah, hell. She needed to get up, needed to be alone to think about how it was that when she was with Jared, she felt...whole. She reached for her clothes, and heard Jared sigh.

"Yeah, we've got to stop meeting like this," she said, hopping into her jeans. "It could get predictable."

"And wouldn't that just be the end of the world as you know it."

In the act of slipping into her shirt, she stopped and faced the gentle sarcasm. He was still sprawled out, sexy as hell, and it took some control not to go back to him. "What does that mean?"

"It means I know. I get it. You don't like to do the same thing more than once, including a guy."

"I did you more than once, didn't I?"

"And now you're running scared."

Ignoring that zing to her heart, she tied her boots. "I'm not running scared, I'm just... Damn it, I told you. I told you what this was."

"Just sex."

"Yes."

"But this isn't just sex, Lily."

"I'm sorry you feel that way." She straightened, hands on her hips. She knew it was a classically aggressive, defensive stance, but she couldn't help herself. She was wearing thin and knew it. "I have things to do."

"I know," he said.

She whirled away, then back. "I'm sorry."

"I know that, too."

She lifted her hands, sank her fingers into her hair. "Then…where does this leave us?"

With a long exhale, he stood and reached for his pants. "I just don't want to be that guy you hooked up with that one summer. The one you smile fondly over but can't remember his name."

Now she sighed, and walked back to him, setting her hands on his chest. "I'm not going to forget your name, Jared."

He covered her hands with his. "Stay with me tonight. In my tent."

Staring down at their joined hands, she thought about how nice that would be. Not just because they could get naked again, but because he could hold her all night, and she would know who she was.

But what about when this was over? Slowly, she shook her head. "I'm sorry." She barely managed to keep it together. "Not yet."

"Lily… I learned the hard way not to put off something that matters. Life is too short for that."

She looked deep into his eyes and knew he knew what he was talking about.

"You matter, Lily," he said quietly. "I know it's been only a short time, but you do. You matter so much."

Oh, God. "Let me catch up." Her hands fell free, and she backed away. Needed to be alone to fall apart. "I really do have to go." She whirled away, then stopped. Turned back, and admitted the truth. "But for what it's worth? You matter, too. More than I wanted you to."

13

LILY CAME AWAKE at dawn to the sound of someone unzipping her tent.

Jared. In reaction, her body tingled, electrified, and without opening her eyes, she stretched, nearly purring at the thought of a quickie before breakfast—

Then she opened her eyes and squeaked in surprise at the face that stuck itself into her tent.

Not Jared.

Jack.

"She's gone," he said, face pale.

"What? Who?"

"Michelle."

She sat up and reached for her clothes. "Define gone."

"As in not here." He shoved his fingers through his hair, his face tight with worry. "Do you think she's just messing with me? Trying to get back at me? Yeah," he said answering his own question, and letting out a ragged breath. "That's probably what she's doing. Right?"

"Jack, tell me what happened."

"She woke me up a while ago, when it was still dark. She said she had to go to the bathroom. I was still sleeping pretty good, so I handed her the flashlight and said go."

"And she went?"

He grimaced. "She said I should come with to protect her. Protect her from what? I said, and she got mad and stomped off. I think I fell back asleep because the next thing I knew, the sun's coming up, and she never came back."

"How long ago did she go, do you think?"

He looked at his watch. "Half an hour, tops. I called for her, and walked around a little bit, but I can't find her. She's probably hiding, just trying to scare me, making me feel guilty. Which is working, by the way."

Lily yanked her sweatshirt over her head. "Except that doesn't really sound like her. Wanting her hair products, yes. Screaming at a frog, yes. Going off into the woods by herself...no."

Jack looked horrified as he nodded his agreement. "And the worst thing? When I got out of the sleeping bag, I tripped over the flashlight. Lily, she never took it with her."

Lily came up to her knees as she wriggled into her jeans. "Give me one minute, I'll be right there."

Jack nodded and left, and Lily let out a breath, telling herself Michelle was fine. She wouldn't have walked off far on her own, she was too nervous out here to do that.

But she hurried out of her tent and went directly to Jared's. "Jared?"

"Yeah. Come in."

His voice was morning gruff, and in another time and place she might have paused to enjoy the innate sexiness of it, but instead she stuck her head into the door.

He was still in his sleeping bag, though the thing had

fallen to low on his hips. He wore no shirt and a rumpled, sleepy-eyed look that heated at the sight of her. "I was dreaming about you," he said, looking as far from the city guy she'd first met as seemed humanly possible.

She let out a breath and tossed him the jeans from near his feet. "I need you."

"Works for me." He tossed the jeans aside and lifted his arms for her to join him, the expression on his face making her thighs quiver, while between them, something else happened entirely.

"Uh, no," she said. "Not that kind of need. Michelle's missing. She went to the bathroom a half an hour ago and hasn't come back."

He was already out of the sleeping bag and grabbing jeans. "Maybe she finally cracked and decided to walk to the nearest mall."

"Yeah, I'd agree," she said, trying not to notice how cute he looked flashing his bare ass as he pulled on his jeans. "Except that whole she-hates-walking thing."

Nodding, he grabbed his boots. "So she's lost?"

"I'm not sure. But I was thinking about that heat-seeking doodad you've got. Could it help?"

"Got it." He dug through his backpack for it, then took her hand. Tugging her close, he gave her a quick kiss on the cheek, then pushed them both out of the tent.

Without hesitation.

She'd had wild sex with him—no, that wasn't right. Even she knew better. They'd made love, twice now, and each time it had been so good, so off-the-charts amazing actually, that he'd connected with her on a level no one else ever had, which in turn had sent her running.

And still, he was there for her, no questions asked. It awed her, stunned her, and when he caught her staring at him, he smiled. "What?"

She could only shake her head. "Let's do this."

HALF OUT OF HIS MIND, Jack waited for Lily, picturing all that could be happening to Michelle with each passing moment. He couldn't believe he hadn't gotten up with her, that he'd let her go by herself. What had he been thinking? He'd been warm and toasty and maybe, just maybe, still a little frustrated, enough to only half listen to her— God. He'd never forgive himself. "I really don't think she's doing this on purpose," he told Lily when she appeared with Jared. "I know she's spoiled sometimes, but…" He'd never felt so sick, so absolutely panicked in his life.

"We'll find her," Lily said, touching his arm. "We will."

Because *not* finding her wasn't an option.

Rock's tent unzipped, but it was Rose's head that stuck out of it. Her hair was wild, her makeup a little smeared, but she was wearing a broad grin that pretty much said exactly what she'd been doing. "Oh my," she said at the sight of Jack, Lily and Jared staring at her. She laughed. "Well, it is a vacation, right?"

Jack wished Michelle was still in his tent, that she looked as rumpled and sated as Rose did right now. And safe.

"Michelle's gone," Lily told her. "She went to the bathroom and didn't come back."

Rose gasped in shock.

"I checked everywhere," Jack told her. "The bathroom stop, the lake, the trail…"

"Ohmigod," Rose whispered. "She's cracked. Probably went looking for the closest mall, poor baby."

"Everyone just stay here, okay?" Lily said. "I'm going to look around, but please, you must stay here." She was looking right at Jack. "Don't make it harder by going off and possibly getting lost yourselves."

Rock stuck his head out of his tent, right next to Rose. He wasn't wearing a shirt. "Are you sure?" he asked. "Because we could all fan out—"

"Not yet," Lily said. "I'm going to check all the close places first before we panic. I'll be right back—"

"I'm coming with you," Jack said.

She took one look at his face and didn't argue. "The rest of you stay here," Lily said.

Rose and Rock nodded, looking unhappy about the command, but not making trouble.

Lily turned to Jared, who stood slightly away from them all, looking down at the PDA unit in his hand, which was equipped with that amazing heat-seeking GPS system. "Jared?"

"A minute." He was working the controls with his thumb, his brow furrowed in concentration.

Lily turned to Jack. "You're sure she said she was going to the bathroom? She didn't say anything else, like maybe she'd had enough and was going to try to get out of here?"

"We all know she'd had enough, but no." He shook his head. "She didn't say anything like that." *Not even good-bye.* "But…"

"But?"

"But I was really asleep, you know?" Dread filled his gut. "And I sleep like the living dead. I wasn't paying her much attention… Oh, God." He scrubbed his hands over his face, then dropped them as he remembered. "Hang on." He dove back into his tent and began going through her bag.

"Jack?" he heard Lily say, speaking through the still flapping tent door. "What are you doing?"

Hitting pay dirt, he found Michelle's makeup bag. Relief flooding him, he stuck his head back out. "If she'd given up and decided to go back on her own, she'd have never left this." But then the truth sank in and his relief abruptly deserted him, because if Michelle hadn't left on purpose, then the situation was even worse.

She *was* lost.

LILY MOVED CLOSE to Jared to look at his small screen. "What do you have?"

"Two possibilities," he said, and everyone moved closer to huddle around him so that Lily had to get on her tiptoes to see the digital display of a satellite map of their area.

Jared pointed to a heat spot. "Us," he said, then widened the screen. A small dot of red appeared to the east, right next to a body of water.

A lake, Lily knew. Not the one right here at camp, but the next alpine lake over, nearly three quarters of a mile away.

Then Jared pointed westward, to the only other heat

spot, which if Lily was reading the satellite correctly, was behind and above them. High above them on the rocks.

Michelle wasn't a climber. Hell, she was barely a hiker. "Jack and I'll check out here," she said, tapping the first red dot. "I think Michelle is more likely to be this one."

Jared nodded. "Okay, but I'll check the other while you're doing that, just to be sure."

"That's pretty much straight up," Lily said. She looked at Jared. "It could be anything, right? A deer, or raccoon?"

He shrugged. "Or a bear, or a mountain cat—" At the collective shocked gasp from Rose, Rock and Jack, he trailed off. "Just saying."

"So basically, anything alive and breathing," Rock said with an exaggerated gulp that under different circumstances, would have been funny on a guy built like he was.

"Anything alive and breathing," Jared agreed. "And emitting body heat, which is to say, not necessarily something we want to run into."

Lily met his gaze as her thoughts whirled. "Okay, so we've got two possibilities. One on a flat, easy-to-walk-to area, the other high up. It's an easy decision, really."

"Oh my God, we have a bear or a mountain cat watching us," Rose said. "Probably just figuring out which of us to eat first." She slipped her hand into Rock's and swallowed hard. "You know he's going to want me." She sucked her lower lip into her mouth. "My body fat ratio is the highest."

Rock slipped an arm around her and pulled her close. "Your body is perfect, and not going to be wild-animal bait, not today."

"No one's going to be animal bait," Lily said firmly. "Because you're all going to stay here and wait while I run to the lake, to that first heat spot. Jack?"

"Right with you. You know, maybe she headed there to wash her face. She loves to wash her face first thing in the morning."

"Why not go to the closer lake, the one that's right here?" Rose asked, and gestured to the lake only several hundred yards away.

"I don't know. But it was dark, really dark, when she got up." Looking exhausted, Jack rubbed his jaw. "And she has a lousy sense of direction. Last night, she asked me how to get to the water, if it was to the right or the left, and when I told her left, I could tell she wasn't listening to me. Maybe she went right on the trail." He looked at Lily. "It could have happened."

Lily agreed. "Let's go right, all the way to the farther lake. If Michelle had kept at it long enough, she'd have indeed ended up there."

"Thing is," Rose said. "She's not one to keep at anything for long."

"Well, she's somewhere," Lily said, determinedly. "And wherever that is, we'll find her." She looked at everyone else. "Wait here. That's the most important part, okay? Wait here. Just yell really loudly if she shows up."

Their camp was a rather secluded, woodsy site, and from the moment Lily and Jack took the trail, they could no longer see the others. The trail to the right was wide, but because they'd not had rain for weeks, the ground was dry and brittle. No noticeable footprints.

"Michelle!" Jack called out from her side every few yards. *"Michelle!"*

The trail climbed a bit, and Jack began to pant for breath. "Gotta tell ya, this one feels too hard. She'd have turned back."

"She's tougher than you think," Lily said. "Michelle! *Michelle, can you hear us?*"

Nothing.

They came to a small creek in a shady aspen grove. The water meandered slowly past them on the left, summer-shallow, and filled with sediment. They both looked at it. "No," Lily said. "She'd not have stopped here to wash her face."

"Oh, no," Jack agreed. "Too dirty. How much farther until the lake?"

"Another quarter of a mile."

They sped up. Jack was panting pretty good at their near-running pace. It was the altitude and nerves, she knew, but he was holding her back. "I'm going ahead," she told him. "Stay on the trail."

Without waiting for a response, she took off, making much better time, and soon enough the trail opened to a clearing, with tawny, undulating wild grass leading directly to a gorgeous beach.

A deserted beach.

The land was vast and rambling, open but not flat, beautiful in its emptiness. The morning light coated the ground with just enough dew to give depth to each individual feature.

Lily scanned the water. Smooth as glass.

And utterly devoid of one spoiled married princess.

But across the lake, there was a single lone deer, sipping from the water, causing the lake to ripple outward in mesmerizing circles.

"A deer," Jack said, coming up behind her, bending at the knees to gasp for breath.

The deer lifted its head, wriggled its nose, then bounded into the woods without a backwards glance.

"And heat spot gone," Jack said, sounding despondent.

Lily looked around, not ready to concede defeat. *"Michelle?"*

No answer, just her own voice echoing back to her. She turned in a slow circle, shoving her sunglasses to the top of her head, scanning every rock, every tree, every inch of the horizon with careful precision.

And it was halfway around, when she was facing dead east, which was the way back to camp, that she saw it. There. High on the craggy rock behind where their camp lay.

A splotch of bright yellow.

What the hell?

Shading her eyes from the morning sun, she squinted and tried to focus in. She recognized the area. Rocky growth, above a dense wooded area.

Above their camp.

Just behind where their camp lay was the makeshift bathroom. They'd set it up against the base of a sharp hill. Which is where she was looking right now. As unbelievable as it seemed, the splash of yellow was halfway up that hill and moving.

As unbelievable as it seemed, Michelle had apparently taken herself on a little climbing expedition. "Uh-oh."

"What? Where is she?" Jack followed her gaze and his jaw dropped. "Is that— *My God.*" He let out a long breath and stared at the moving dot of yellow. "What the hell is she doing?" He brought his hands up to his mouth, cupping them around his lips. "Michelle!"

"Don't," Lily breathed, grabbing his arm. "Don't startle her."

Regardless, they were too far away to see if Michelle had reacted to Jack's voice. Dropping his hands, he whirled back the way they'd come.

Together they raced through the woods and back into camp, where a startled Rose and Rock, standing by the fire, looked up.

"Did you find her?" Rose asked.

"Is she okay?" Rock rushed to ask.

"We found her, we just haven't gotten to her yet." Lily kept moving through camp toward the yellow spot that she could no longer see, not from here. "Where's Jared?"

"He went after the other heat spot," Rose said.

The one that had turned out to be Michelle after all. Lily skidded to a halt and stared at her. "I told him to stay."

"Honey, most men don't know how to take directions, you know?"

No. No, she didn't know but she was coming to. It didn't matter now. She was going to get him, and Michelle, and then she was going to put her hands around their necks and squeeze.

And then...

And then, if Jared was up for it, she was going to hug him to death, just to finish him off. "Come on," she said to Jack, and headed east. Soon they stood in the low valley, with sharp, jagged, sheer rock on either side, climbing up hundreds of feet. She'd been here earlier, and hadn't seen Michelle, but then again, she wouldn't have if Michelle had gone climbing. The shrubbery and lodgepole pines and scrub blocked most of the rock so that seeing any distance upward became all but impossible.

There was the fallen log, the group of three trees that they all had used for shelter when going to the bathroom in the woods without four walls and a lock.

"What do you think?" Jack asked, his eyes a little wild with worry and fear. "She start climbing from here?"

Hard to tell. The dirt here was dry and brittle as well. There were no defined or clear footprints, but lots of dust disturbed from all of them from the night before, and, Lily hoped Michelle from this morning. All the comingled trampling led back to camp.

Except…

Cocking her head, she studied the narrow path that led straight up. Not exactly a path, but it was definitely a route she would have chosen if she was alone, and especially if she wanted to remain alone.

From up there on the rock precipice, she'd be able to see far and wide. But better yet, no one would be able to see her. Maybe just what she'd have wanted on a day like this, if she was a woman not sure about where she and her husband were going to go with their marriage.

Jared had thought of that, too. And he'd gone after her.

Damn it.

Her heart started to pound. He was no more equipped than Michelle to make that climb. God. If he got hurt, she was going to kill him.

14

"JACK," Lily called out, head still tilted up, still trying to see.

"Yeah?" he asked from behind her.

She gestured up. "I'm going to climb it."

Jack eyed the rock wall and the outcropping that was cut out and so overgrown with bushes that they couldn't see above it. *"Where?"*

"Here." Lily began to climb the rock using questionable foot and hand holds.

"Lily, I don't think Michelle could have…"

She didn't waste the breath to respond, and a minute later heard him scrambling behind her to keep up, his breath rasping in and out of his lungs.

"This is all my fault," he said, panting. "I was so frustrated that she really believed I loved her for her daddy's money. I kept taking that out on her. God, I've been such an ass."

"It's not all your fault." Lily glanced up, but could still see nothing. "Michelle! Michelle, can you hear me?"

She wanted to lay her eyes on Jared, too, right now, right this minute. Honestly, what had he been thinking, going off to play hero?

Finally, she got to the top and crawled over. Normally the view would take her breath. She could see everything in a captivating, panoramic circle: the sharp jagged mountains lined with blankets and blankets of green, the dips and valleys of rock, the myriads of small alpine lakes like ribbons of blue.

It was staggeringly gorgeous.

Then she saw something even more gorgeous. Jared stepping out from behind a tree, hair tousled, jaw streaked with dirt, shirt torn, a knee bleeding…

Yeah. Staggeringly gorgeous.

And her heart simply turned over and exposed its belly. Oh, God. No. No, not this man. She was not going to fall for this man.

Too late, whispered a little voice inside her head. *Far too late.*

It had already been a monumentally bad morning, the worst, and after being on the edge for close to an hour, and now teetering on a different edge altogether, she didn't feel steady, so when he lifted his hand, in which he held his PDA, with a sheepish smile on his face, she nearly lost it right then, but somehow she kept it together.

Then Jack was there beside her yelling, "Michelle! *Michelle, where are you?*"

"Here." Michelle came out from behind a second tree, a spot of bright yellow in her jacket, her hair loose and tumbling around her shoulders, a cut along her jaw, but otherwise whole and healthy.

Jack rushed to her and hauled her in for a tight hug, fisting his hands at her back as if he was never going to let her go. "*What was that?* Where were you going? What were you doing?"

"Just trying to get a good view," she said, sounding shaken. "I wanted to do something for myself, and prove I could. So I got up here, and then I was afraid to go back down."

"Oh, baby—"

"I'm so sorry, Jack, I didn't mean to scare you."

He pulled back to stare at her. He let out a low laugh, then hauled her close again. "It's okay. I love you, Michelle. Love you so damn much."

Lily's eyes had locked on Jared and didn't let go as she moved toward him.

"She's okay," Jared said, gesturing to Michelle.

"Yes, but how about you?" It was hard to breathe, but that didn't matter. "Looking a little worse for wear there, chief."

He lifted a shoulder. "I'm fine."

"You helped her get up here, to the top."

"A little."

A lot, she suspected.

"She wanted a taste of freedom," he said. "Wanted to be in charge of her own destiny. Not because of her father, or because of her husband, but because of herself."

A feeling Lily knew all too well. As, she suspected, did Jared. Being in charge of one's destiny had to mean a lot to a man who hadn't always gotten to be in charge of his. She'd meant to strangle him, possibly kill him, but now…but now she wanted something else entirely.

He smiled. "What?"

"What what?"

"You're looking at me funny. Like…"

Like I want to spread you on a cracker? Because I do…

"Like maybe…" He stepped even closer, so that they were toe to toe and eye to eye. Or they would have been eye to eye if she'd been just over six feet tall as he was, instead she was more like nose to chest, but he dipped his head down a little so that their jaws nearly brushed. She could feel his warm breath on her temple, his gaze running over her face, and it was the oddest thing.

She felt naked in front of a crowd.

"You were worried about me," he said softly, sounding a little surprised, even awed and a lot amused.

"Hell yeah, I was worried."

He grinned, and the sight of it caused a flood of emotions: fear, relief—giddy relief…anger. "You think it's funny?" she demanded. "That I was so worried I could barely breathe?"

"Are you kidding? I—"

But she didn't want to hear it, and whirled away, leaving him talking to air.

He merely snagged her arm, bringing her back around to face him. At least he was wise enough to swipe the grin off his face. "It's sweet," he said. "I think you're incredibly sweet."

"You keep calling me that."

"Yeah? So?"

"No one's ever accused me of being sweet before."

At that, he tipped back his head and laughed, and, oh yeah, that pissed her off, too, but he scrambled to tighten his hands on her before she tore free again. "Here's the thing," he said. "It's not an insult."

She glared at him, or wanted to, but her chest felt too big, and sort of restricted, and for some odd reason, her eyes and throat burned. "We're behind schedule," she managed. "Let's go."

Michelle and Jack were still kissing as if they intended to swallow each other's tongues. She stalked past, tapping them on the shoulders as she went. "Reunion's over. We've got a hike to finish."

THEY MOVED eight miles that day. By the time night came, and Lily got everyone fed and happy, she was feeling the effects of keeping a smile on her face.

Over a roaring fire, Rose suggested a game of Truth or Dare. Rock nixed that, probably with a healthy dose of fear of what Rose might ask him to do or say.

Jack, going through the supplies that had been dropped for them earlier, came up with a bottle of whiskey, which he used to liberally lace everyone's hot chocolate.

They all sipped, then promptly choked in unison as the fiery stuff made its way to their bellies. Jack grinned and stood up. "Okay, here's a game from the college drinking days. We go around the circle and tell something about ourselves. Either a truth or a lie... Everyone has to guess which. If you fool everyone, then they all have to drink. If you don't, then the liar drinks."

"We'll be plastered in no time." Rose clapped with glee. "I love it."

Jack nodded. "Good." He sat next to Michelle and poured a second, very healthy dose of whiskey into his own mug. "I'll give you an example of how it works."

He looked at Michelle. "Truth or lie...me going out with you had nothing to do with your father being richer than God."

"Lie," Michelle whispered.

Jack, eyes never leaving hers, lifted his mug to his mouth and took a long swig.

Everyone at the campfire was silent as the implications of what Jack had said, and then admitted was a lie, sank in.

He wiped his mouth with the back of his hand. "Okay, so now you get the game."

Michelle stared morosely into her mug, silent.

Jack looked at her. "Now I'll go again to be first," he said. "Truth or lie... By the end of our first date, I didn't give a shit about your father's money."

"Lie," she whispered, head down, eyes on her drink.

"Truth," Jack whispered, then pointed to everyone's mug. "You all drink."

They lifted their spiked hot chocolate to their lips and each took a healthy swallow, while Michelle just stared at Jack. "What? What did you just say?"

"By the end of our first date," he repeated softly. "I didn't give a shit about your father's money." He nudged her mug to her lips. "I haven't given it a single thought since then."

Michelle drank, then coughed, her eyes watering as she continued to stare at Jack. "Really?"

He sank next to her, and smiled a little shakily. "Really."

"Oh, Jack." She flung her arms around her husband, the action touching Lily more deeply than she'd expected. Or maybe it was the two deep sips of spiked hot chocolate she'd had. She glanced at Jared.

He was looking right at her.

Nope, not the alcohol getting to her head.

Him.

"Okay, now me." Rose stood up, a little unsteady on her feet. "Truth or lie." she cupped her own breasts. "I know my body's fabulous, but it's not quite all God-given."

Rock let his gaze travel slowly up said body, from her toes to her roots and slowly back again. "No, ma'am," he said. "That's all you."

"Fooled you." Rose locked her gaze on his and pushed up her breasts. "Sometimes God needs a little help."

They all drank, then Rock pulled her to the log and stood up. He looked down at Rose. "You're far too much of a handful for me."

Rose's smile faded. "Truth."

Rock paused, then smiled. "Gotcha. You drink."

Rose laughed heartily, drank along with everyone else, then hauled Rock back down and laid her lips on his.

Lily looked into her drink. All around her...romance, love—

Jared turned to her. "Should I go next?"

"Sure," she said as casually as she could, but still her heart began to race.

He stood, then looked down at her. "I'm having the time of my life."

Lily found her lips curving. "Even with diving over cliffs and climbing other cliffs and—"

"Even with," he said. "Maybe especially with."

"Well, that's just crazy enough to be the truth," she said, and because he hadn't fooled her, *he* took a long swig of his laced hot chocolate.

Lily drew a deep breath and stood up. "Okay, here goes. I'm adventurous on the outside—"

"Well, duh," Michelle said with a smile. "You're not fooling anyone, Lily."

"—but on the inside," she said, "on the inside, especially with my own heart, I'm far too careful."

Jared tipped his head up and looked at her, his indescribable eyes clear and open on hers. "Things can change, Lily. People can change."

"You're supposed to say truth or lie," she whispered.

Jared shook his head. "You know you can change it."

"Jared."

"Damn it, truth. *Your* truth."

She lifted her mug and drank. Hell, everyone lifted their mugs and drank. People were starting to get some damn silly grins on their faces. Rose topped off her mug, drank it down, then staggered to her feet. Reaching a hand out to Rock, she tried to wink at him, but ended up just opening and shutting both eyes, which cracked her up. "Stick a fork in me, I'm done. Take me to bed, cowboy."

Rock surged to his feet so fast, Lily's head spun. Slipping an arm around Rose, he led her toward her tent, chuckling as she walked with the care of the very cautious, or the very inebriated.

Jack pulled Michelle to her feet then, too, and pushed her hair out of her eyes. "If I wasn't drunk, I'd carry you to bed."

Oh, Lily thought, watching Michelle smile, a real

smile, they were going to work it out. They were going
to get their happily ever after. It made her sigh with hap-
piness for them.

"If I was drunker," Michelle whispered to Jack. "I'd
actually believe there was a bed in our tent."

He smiled. "We don't need a bed."

She grinned dreamily, and hugged him. "Oh, Jack."

Lily watched them go, an unnameable yearning
welling within her. She'd never really longed for a
husband. She'd liked being on her own, strong and independent.

But…but then she'd sort of lost her footing. She
thought maybe she'd found it, or she was beginning to,
and now…now she felt different. Not as strong on the
outside, no doubt. But on the inside…maybe stronger.
At least strong enough to admit that there was no
denying she was longing for a partner, for someone to
complement her life in the best possible way.

Jared took her hand. "How about it? Can I convince
you I have a bed in my tent?"

She tried to laugh but it was hard with the odd lump
in her throat.

Jared tipped up her chin, studying her face in that
way he had of seeing all the way into her. But she felt
just a little too raw, a little too exposed at that moment,
so she turned away, and then to her surprise tripped over
her own toes. "Whoops," she said, and would have
landed flat on her face if Jared hadn't slipped an arm
around her, catching her up against him.

"Whoa," he said, and turned her in his arms to face
him. "Hello."

"I'm not drunk, I barely had any of the whiskey."

"Then maybe you just like being against me."

"Maybe I do," she admitted. "Good thing you have fast reflexes."

He ran his hands down her back. "I have a feeling fast reflexes are required with you."

She smiled, then found it clogged with that lump in her throat as her eyes unexpectedly filled.

"Ah, Lily," he said softly, and cupped her cheek. "What is it?"

"I need to put out the campfire."

"Lily."

"Truth?"

"Please."

"We only have one night left."

"Doesn't have to be only one night left."

She looked up into his eyes and saw so many things; lovely, terrifying things. "I don't want you to get hurt," she whispered.

"I'm a big boy. I can handle whatever comes."

"And you have. I know."

"So what's the problem?"

She opened her mouth, then closed it again. What was the problem? Was it having such a warm, smart and sexy man want to be with her? Was she that big an idiot?

"I want to spend time with you in the real world, Lily."

She lifted her hands, gestured all around them. "This is the real world. My world."

"Okay, let me clarify. I want to spend time with you in any world: yours, mine…doesn't matter. Let's go out."

"On a date?"

"Yeah."

"Define date."

"I pick you up, we laugh and have fun, maybe make-out…and then we do it all over again another night."

"Sounds simple."

"Sounds good."

Oh, God, it did. "We've only known each other a few days."

"Days. Years. Seconds. You can't put a time line on these things, Lily."

She stared at him. "If I keep guiding, I'll be gone a lot. I won't have time…"

"Then we see each other when you are around."

"There might be weeks in between."

"Yes, but see, there's these newfangled contraptions called phones, e-mail, text messaging— In fact, I know a guy who has everything you could ever need." He grinned. "I'll hook you up."

He looked so earnest, so sincere, her breath caught. "Jared."

He smiled. "Admit it. You like me."

Yeah, she did. Way too much. "Look, here's the truth."

"Finally."

"I've never been too successful at this dating thing. I don't know why really, except I've never been too fond of ties. They…choke me."

"Me too. It's why I don't wear suits to the office any-more."

"Jared."

"Lily."

She could only shake her head. "You're not listening…"

"Yes, I am. You're trying to dump me."

"I'm trying to be honest with you. I've never had much time for doing the long-term dating thing, and I'm trying to tell you that while this has been nice—"

"Great," he corrected. "It's been great."

She stared at him, then had to concede. "Okay, yeah. Great. While this has been great—" She broke off when he smiled, rather full of himself, and she had to laugh. "You're awfully hard to dump."

"I'm hoping to be. Look, not to rain on your parade here, but why are you doing this now?" He stepped close, so that she could see the mesmerizing mix of jade and chocolate in his eyes, so that she could smell him, that yummy soap, whatever it was, and him. "We have one more night," he said, and waggled his eyebrows suggestively. "I mean, why not take advantage of me for that, and then dump me tomorrow?"

She eyed him warily. "You're going to be okay with me dumping you tomorrow?"

"Hell, no. But maybe by then I'll have thought of something to keep you indebted to me. Maybe I'll help you save someone or something. Hell, maybe I'll save you."

He shot her a cocky-boy smile so filled with humor and affection, she couldn't speak for a minute. "Save me from what?"

Still smiling, he just looked at her, all rugged and sexy, and just like that, another piece of her heart fell into place. "Damn it," she whispered, and touched his mouth. "You turn me upside down."

"Well then, consider us even."

She stared into his eyes. "I don't know what I'm doing. Not even a little bit."

"You're complicating things, that's why."

"No. No, I'm not. I like things decidedly uncomplicated. Which is why I'm going to walk away right now."

His smile faded. "Lily, don't."

Oh, God, she had to. It was what she did, walk away, rather than get attached. Right? "I'm sorry." A tear escaped. Damn it. That was the *last* one. "Good night, Jared."

She carefully put out the campfire, dousing the flames, covering the hot embers with sand until nothing smoked. She moved to her tent, then feeling the pull of Jared's gaze, turned to look at him over her shoulder.

One more night.

He was right, why would she walk away now?

He slid his hands into his pockets, rocking back on his heels, looking both sexy and adorably unsure.

And why did that float her boat? Why did she want to nibble that rough jaw and slide her hands beneath his loose T-shirt to find that warm, hard body beneath?

One more night...

Oh yeah, she wanted that one more night, she really did, and without letting any more thoughts cloud her judgment, she held out her hand, her entire body coming to life when he started walking toward her.

One more night...

It would be enough. It would.

"I should tell you," she said when he came close and took her hand. "I have a little problem admitting when I'm wrong."

"Ah." He nodded seriously, but a smile had come into his eyes. "So how are you going to play this?" He toyed with a strand of her hair. "Obviously, you've decided you want me for one more night." He looked at her for a beat. "And yet you can't say so because that would make you feel foolish, and we all know, looking foolish doesn't suit you… Hmm, this is a tough one."

She had to laugh at how he'd painted her—which was as accurate as could be. "Maybe I could…"

"Yes? I'm all ears."

"I could show you," she whispered, wondering how it was she felt like both laughing and crying. She pressed her body up to his. "Like this."

"You know, that's a good start." He pretended to resist, but when she slid her hands down his back, he drew in a shuddery breath and sighed against her hair. "I think I'm going to like the whole showing-me thing."

"I thought so." Unzipping her tent, she pulled him inside.

15

JARED WATCHED Lily zip her tent, closing them inside, alone. He could feel the beat of time passing in tune with the beat of his heart, and understood that this might be it.

His last time with her.

It took away all the teasing tone to his voice, and left nothing but stark, naked need. "Lily—"

She dropped to her knees and went for the buttons on his pants, but he stilled her fingers and hit his knees as well, bringing their joined hands to his heart.

"Kiss me," she whispered.

Pulling her closer, he lowered his head and took her mouth, kissing one corner first, and then the other, and then finally taking it home, slipping his tongue inside to find hers.

A soft hum of pleasure escaped her, and egged him on. He opened his mouth wider, taking more of her, needing even more than that, but she gave it all to him. Lips and tongue and teeth, until he was doing a slow burn for her.

It took all of two seconds.

"Jared," she whispered, arching into him, her hands, restless and hungry, running over his back. A soft, shuddering sigh escaped her. "More."

Yeah, he wanted more, too. Needed more. But this wasn't going to be a quickie. No hot and fast fire that could burn out in a flash. No, if this was it, then he planned to linger, to make her his, so that she would never, ever forget him.

Pressing her back onto her sleeping bag, he bent over her, taking his time, kissing her lips, her throat, her collarbone, and back up again, but her hands kept shoving at his clothes, trying to rush him. To stop that from happening, he gathered her wrists and stretched them over her head, holding her still while he looked down at her.

Her mouth was wet from his, and as he watched, she licked her lips, as if needing that last taste of him. God, her mouth, it was made for this, for him, and he bent for another slow, deep, wet kiss, keeping at her until he felt all resistance fall away. Until he was aching and she was panting for breath, giving into him with a soft, desperate murmur that was the most erotic sound he'd ever heard. She was moving against him, restless, her breasts rubbing his chest, her legs entangled in his, and all he wanted to do was sink into her. Stunned by how fast his control was slipping, he shook his head. "Lily, I—"

She reared up and bit his lower lip.

Heat shot straight through him, pooling at his erection. And any vestige of control vanished like a rug being jerked out from beneath his feet. "God, Lily."

"Hurry."

Hurry, like they always did, rushing to the big bang, which was so amazing with her, it was like an addictive drug. "Not tonight," he said. Her white bra shimmered in the dark. He flicked open the front clasp and spread the material away from her. Her nipples were already hard. "For once we're not going to hurry."

Hands still above her head, she arched up. "But I want you."

"And you're going to have me." He dipped his head to taste his way down her throat. "All night long."

"No one has that much stamina—ohmigod," she gasped when he licked a pebbled nipple, then sucked it into his mouth.

"We can always start again," he said against her skin. He could be with her like this for a hundred years and not get tired of the feel of her, the taste, the scent, and staggered by the thought, he closed his eyes and breathed her in. "A couple of times, whatever it takes."

"Whatever it takes," she repeated with a choked laugh as he kissed his way to her other breast. "You sound like you know what you're doing."

"When it comes to you, Lily, I think I do."

"You can't say that. We haven't known each other long enough. This is just—"

He slid a hand between her thighs and she sucked in a breath as she opened them for him. "Sex?" he asked softly.

She gasped when he stroked his hands unerringly over the denim. "You know it's supposed to be light and casual between us. We've talked about it."

"*You've* talked about it," he said, and bent to her breasts again. "Me, not so much."

"But…" She blinked rapidly, as if she needed to in order to see past the sexual haze that surrounded them.

Good. At least he wasn't alone in losing his mind.

"So you're saying this isn't just…"

"Hell, no. Not for me, and if you're being honest, not for you either." He curled his tongue around a nipple while his hand skimmed down her rising and falling belly, slipping into the waistband of her jeans.

She sucked in a breath to give him better access. "Jared…we're wearing too many clothes."

Lifting up, he tugged her pants off, tossed them over his shoulder, leaving her gloriously bare.

She squirmed, then shot him up a little smile. "Now *you're* wearing too many clothes."

"We'll get there. I like you naked, Lily. I like the smooth feel of your skin…" He stroked a hand over her ribs, rasped a thumb over a nipple. "And I love the scent of you." He stroked a thumb over her wet, hot center, making her gasp and rock her hips for more.

"When I'm with you," she managed. "I don't know if I'm coming or going."

"Oh, you're coming." He slid a finger into her while his thumb made another passing sweep over her creamy flesh. "You're going to come again and again and again…"

"*Jared—*"

"Right here." With each stroke of that thumb, she rocked her hips against him, urging him into her rhythm, but he was already right there with her. Damn, she was hot. Hot and wet, and *his*. He was crazy to want her this way, a woman who'd just as soon never face the undeniable growing emotions they had for each other, even after only a few days.

But he did. He wanted her for always.

Hell of a fix, given that she'd run for the hills if she knew his thoughts. So he kissed her deep. He had his tongue inside her mouth, his fingers inside her body, was as close to her as he could get, and yet, it wasn't enough. Hell, they could do this every night until they were old and gray and he had a feeling it wouldn't be enough.

Because he loved her.

"Jared...please. Please, now."

"Yeah, now." He stroked her again, heat coiling low in his belly when she gasped his name like a prayer, a mantra.

He definitely liked the sound of that, and let himself look at her, soak her in. Her eyes were closed, her hair wild around her face, falling around her pillow like shiny silk. Her mouth was open, as if she needed it that way just to breathe, and with her head back, her throat was exposed.

He'd never seen anything more beautiful in his life.

Leaning over her, he put his mouth to her neck. She sighed, the soft sound going straight to his gut.

And lower.

Her hands came up to his shoulders, running restlessly down his back as she murmured some wordless plea.

She wanted him. She wanted him inside her, and maybe, just maybe, she wanted inside *him,* too.

He kissed his way to her shoulder, then a breast, and she cried out his name in a voice he knew would headline his dreams for the rest of his life. Beneath the hands he had on her, he felt her muscles tense and tremble, felt her hips rocking with pure, mindless pleasure.

She was close.

He nudged her over with his fingers, feeling the tension rumble through her, which was erotic as hell, but not nearly as erotic as the taste of her, he knew, so he dipped his head and put his mouth on her. And she fell again, the sharp edge of her pleasure nearly taking him with her.

While she still shuddered, he kicked off a boot. "Condom."

"Inside there," she gasped, and pointed to a zippered pouch on her pack.

He had the packet in his teeth, and was trying to lose his other boot and pull off his shirt at the same time.

"Jared?"

Damn it, he had a knot in his damn bootlace. "Yeah?"

Her hair was wild about her face, which was flushed. Her body, sprawled out beneath him, was damp and dewy, and the most mouthwatering thing he'd ever seen. "How about now? Can you hurry now?"

He'd never laughed while being hard enough to pound a nail through stone. "I swear I'm trying." Finally he got his boot off, and she helped him with his jeans, taking a second to glide her tongue along his length, leaving him a quivery mess of sensation, and then…oh, God…and finally, *finally,* he pushed her back, rose over her, and thrust home.

She was hot, slick and so ready for him, he nearly came right then. There had to be a name for this, he thought dimly, this mind-blowing sensation he felt being inside her, feeling her breathe with him, her heart in sync with his.

Oh, wait. There *was* a name for it. *Love.* "Lily."

Arching up, she wrapped her legs around his waist, sending him even deeper within her, so damned deep he could happily drown. Her fingers dug into his buttocks now, urging him on. Her hips were rocking, her muscles tightening on him as she came again, or still, it didn't matter because she was taking him with her into the wild current, and there was nothing he could do to stop it.

"So good," she murmured, her breasts pressed hard to his chest, her mouth working its way along his jaw, her breath scraping in and out of her lungs, panting in his ear now. He could feel her heart beating, or maybe that was his. Yes, that was his. He ground himself against her with every thrust, latching his mouth onto her neck and holding on, staking his claim, sinking his teeth into her skin as he…completely…lost…it, wondering if he would even live through it.

From some dim recess in his mind, he felt her go over, and then he heard himself say it, the words he could no longer hold back. "I love you, Lily…"

And then he let himself fall.

LILY OPENED her eyes. She was cradled against a hard, damp chest. *Nice.* Limp as a noodle, she slowly floated back to earth—

And then remembered.

Had he really said—

No.

No, he hadn't uttered those three little words. She'd only imagined them, dreamt them up while coming so hard her toes were still curled.

How was it possible that this kept happening between them, that each and every time got more intimate, more deep, in fact so deep that she couldn't imagine being without him?

Good thing then, that this was their last night, wasn't it? Yeah, definitely best just to stay right here, in the moment, and she pressed closer to his big, warm body, thinking in the moment was a pretty damn fine place to be…and let herself drift off.

WHEN JARED OPENED his eyes, dawn was just a pink-and-purple ribbon in the sky. He was wrapped up warm and toasty in Lily, which suited him. He pulled her close and breathed her in.

In her sleep, she cuddled closer, putting her face into the crook of his neck and letting out a soft hum of pleasure, her body far ahead of her brain in the accepting-him department.

He just hoped to God her brain caught up with the rest of things soon.

As in today soon.

With a soft sigh, Lily opened her eyes. "I had a dream that you said…"

"Yeah. It wasn't a dream."

She blinked once, slowly, and then he felt her body tense as she sat up.

The loss of her body heat was nothing compared to the gaping hole he felt in his heart when she backed from him. "Look," he said. "I know. I get it. This is scary shit."

"Only because you changed things."

"Change doesn't have to be bad."

She let out a mirthless laugh. "Tell that to my old career."

He was quiet a moment. "You're not the only one who's faced big changes this year."

She immediately softened. "I know," she said, touching him. "God, I know."

"If I managed to change my ways, the original workaholic, to an extremely different lifestyle, trust me. You can do anything, including be whole and happy with a different job, with any job, with people in your life—"

"People? Or you?"

"Hell yeah, me."

She stared at him for one beat, then began searching the tent. On her hands and knees, she kept her back to him, which was a damn fine view, but not the one he wanted. "Lily, your entire life has been about taking risks. This is just one more in a long line of many. And actually, a helluva lot safer than most—"

His shirt hit him in the face. When he pulled it free, she was searching for the rest of his clothes. She patted the sleeping bag, finding her jeans but not his, then looked at the zipper of her tent, which had been pulled, but not the horizontal one, and with all their…physical exertion, some things inadvertently been shoved outside.

Mainly his pants.

"Sorry." She was so sorry she shoved his boots out after them. He'd have pointed that out but she had that look on her face, the look of a woman heading directly toward Panicville but trying desperately to maintain an illusion of calm.

"Better go get them," she said.

With a sigh, he brushed past her, sticking his head and bare torso outside.

The sky had lightened now, to a pale baby blue. His jeans had actually made their way far enough from the tent that he couldn't reach them from the safety of inside. Didn't that figure? He was going to start the day bare-ass naked outside. He hoped nothing would freeze off.

One quick look around assured him he was alone, and he slipped out of the tent. *Naked.* Behind him, he heard the zipper, and turned just in time to watch it slide down, shutting him out.

The equivalent of being shoved out the proverbial front door after a bad date.

Only this hadn't been a bad date. Nothing had gone wrong at all, except his mouth had gone off without written permission from his brain and he'd let his feelings slip.

He figured since he'd been in the throes of an orgasm at the time, he should be given a break, but that wasn't going to happen. Damn, it was chilly, he thought, bending for his jeans. Goose bumps rose over every naked inch of him.

From behind came a rustle, then a gasp and a low *whoa-baby* whistle.

Wincing, he turned, and faced a grinning Rose. He held his shirt and pants over himself.

"Well, good morning there, cowboy," she all but purred.

Perfect. He did his best not to squirm, but that proved difficult as she lapped him up with her eyes as though he was a bowl of spilled milk.

"I knew it," she said silkily. "I knew you were hiding an amazing body beneath those clothes of yours. Hot damn, I was right."

Jared wished it wasn't quite so cold. He wanted to dive into his tent, but to do so, he would have to go prancing right past her nose, his bare ass frozen solid.

The polite thing for her to do, of course, would be to vanish back inside her tent and give him a moment of privacy.

But Rose wasn't interested in giving him a moment of privacy. "You had a nice evening, I take it," she said with a waggle of her eyebrows, running her gaze very frankly over him.

Then, above her head, appeared Rock. He took in the situation with a good amount of amused sympathy. "Let the guy go by, Rose."

"Ah, but you're no fun."

"Come on, I'll show you some fun." With a nod to Jared, Rock pulled Rose back into their tent.

"Oh, Rock," he heard her sigh with pleasure. "Oh, now *there's* a most excellent way to distract me."

Jared sighed, too, not exactly filled with pleasure because the cold air was seeping into parts unknown, and he had a feeling, despite his wishes to the contrary, he'd just been unceremoniously and officially dumped.

16

It was their last day. The thought never left Lily's mind as she led the group through Alpine Pass, slowly making their way back to the trailhead where they'd begun four days earlier.

It went well, even if Lily didn't absorb anything they did, not the trail, nor the rugged peaks all around her, nor the way the river sparkled and raced at their side.

Jared loved her.

Loved.

Her.

She understood the concept. Hell, she'd even seen it up close and personal. Hadn't her parents been in and out of love all her life? Hadn't her friends found love, then occasionally lost it, and if they were particularly into torture, found it again?

It was all around her.

But she'd never imagined it happening to her. Had never really wanted it to. Her life had been adventurous and wild enough, without adding that to the mix.

Behind her Michelle and Jack held hands. At the beginning of this trek they'd been barely speaking, and now they couldn't stop staring into each other's eyes.

She didn't give herself any credit for that. The mountains and the air and the sheer glory of the Sierras had done it. That, and some damn hard work and understanding on their part.

But somehow, it was just a little painful to look at them now.

What did that say about her, that she'd been able to enjoy them more when their relationship had been in trouble? It said she was a bitch, that's what. She sighed and kept moving.

Rose laughed at something Rock said, and Lily smiled a little grimly. Rose had confided in her that Rock had been a fabulous diversion, just the extra fun she'd needed on this trip, but when it was over, it was over.

Now see, *there* was a woman after her own heart. Lily glanced at Rock, who didn't look nearly as happy and carefree as Rose, or nearly as happy and carefree as he'd started out being four days ago.

Seemed Lily wasn't the only moper around here.

She felt for Rock, she did, but damn it, hadn't Rose laid out the ground rules, making him understand that fun was fun, and now that fun had to be over?

Bringing up the rear was Jared. She could feel his presence without looking at him. Mostly because in spite of her best efforts, her heart had been snagged by his.

Damn him.

She hadn't wanted ties. Strings. Attachments. She'd been only looking to find herself. And she'd said so, too. She hadn't wanted anything more than a couple of beautiful nights, which they'd had.

But—and here's where it got tricky—somewhere

along the way, things *had* changed. *She* had changed.
She'd realized she wasn't the same woman she'd been,
and she probably never would be again.

But it didn't mean she wasn't strong. Strength could
come from within, she'd learned that firsthand. She *was*
strong. Just not the type of woman to want a forever
with a man. "Damn it."

"That's the third or fourth time you've muttered that
to yourself."

Startled, she looked up into Jared's hazel gaze. He'd
come up alongside her, and she'd been so busy analyz-
ing and stressing, she hadn't even heard him.

He didn't shoot her his trademark grin, and she felt
compelled to say something, anything. "Jared—"

But he kept walking. A little stunned, she slowed to
stare after him.

"Oooh, look," Rose called out, and pointed to the
alpine meadow that had just opened up in front of them.
"A place to take a break— Ohmigod, check it out!"

She pointed to a high ridge, and they all looked up
at the five big-horned bucks watching them, their taupe
coats blending perfectly with the talus slopes. Beyond
them, on a sheer fringe of rock, the sun created halos
around their magnificent heads.

"Wow," Jack said to Michelle. "Your dad would sure
love to be here with his long-range."

"If my daddy shot Bambi, I'd never forgive him."

"Not Bambi," Lily said. "Those are big boys, not
babies. But I'm glad no one's here taking shots."

"What are they doing?" Michelle whispered, as if the
deer could hear them from all the way across the valley.

"They're just watching us silly humans walk," Lily said, "in *their* woods."

Silly, and *stupid* she silently added, not looking at Jared. God, she hated to be wrong.

And she *was* wrong, about so many things. Too bad she wasn't any good at admitting that.

They walked some more, and after a while, stopped for lunch.

"It's so beautiful," Michelle said with awe, sitting on a rock eating a sandwich, for once her yellow rain gear nowhere in sight. "All of it."

It was. The air was so clear and crisp they could see each individual jagged edge on the rocks. The river widened into yet another of the hundreds of small lakes in the area, and thanks to the rocky cliffs jutting high into the sky, shadowed by a thick growth of lodgepole pines and bush, the place was a little spot of heaven.

They begged Lily to start a little campfire so they could make s'mores with the last of the chocolate. She got a small fire going, then glanced over at Jared.

He'd moved away from her, staring into the water.

Well, damn it. Didn't he know that this was all *his* fault? Throwing around those three little words that were guaranteed to strike terror into any woman's heart—

Okay, *her* heart.

"Look." Rock pointed to one of the tallest redwoods, where a huge rope swing had been set up.

"Careful," Lily said. "We should check—"

But Rock had kicked off his shoes, grabbed the rope and took a flying leap.

"—the rope," Lily finished with a sigh.

Rock's momentum took him high over the water, where, with a loud "Woo-hoo" he let go with wild abandon, and hit the water with a huge splash.

Jared went next.

Jack quickly moved to join them.

"But your clothes—" Michelle began, then when Jack surfaced in the water, she just sighed. She had a sweet smile on her face. "Oh, well."

"Come in," he called, and splashed her.

It didn't take much to convince her.

Or Rose.

Jared climbed out of the water, leaving the two happy couples engaged in a water fight. Standing on the shore, his back to Lily, he shook the water from his head like a shaggy dog, then pulled off his shirt.

Lily stared at the sleek muscles in his back and was nearly overcome by the urge to put her hands on him. And not just to jump his long, lean, wet bones either, although there was a good amount of that urge, as well, but also something far deeper.

She just wanted to be close, as close as possible: talking, laughing, hiking, naked or clothed…

It pissed her off.

Stalking over to him, she stood at his side and put her hands on her hips, staring into the water where the others were still playing with wild abandon. "I'd like to know what you meant by throwing that *L*-word around."

He turned his head and looked at her, and damn if behind the hurt and frustration, he wasn't laughing at her. "*L*-word?"

"Yes."

"There are a lot of *L*-words out there," he said. "Maybe you should be a little bit more specific."

"You know exactly which *L*-word I'm talking about."

Arching an eyebrow, he looked down at her with that smile on his lips, the one that wasn't quite real because it didn't reach his eyes.

"Love," she reminded him. "You said you love me."

"And this thrilled the hell out of you."

"Love doesn't fit into my life, and you know it." She felt thrown, seriously thrown. Why hadn't he gotten pissed off and run screaming from her? Why was he still standing here talking to her, looking at her in a way that made breathing all but a forgotten art?

"Why not?" he asked very quietly. "Why don't you, for once and all, come right out and tell me why love doesn't fit into your life."

"Well, because…" He was looking at her patiently, waiting for logic, when she had absolutely none. "Crap," she said brilliantly, and crossed her arms over her chest.

He just looked at her, his disappointment palpable. "It's okay," he finally said. "I understand."

And he dove back into the water, nothing but a ripple in the water as he vanished beneath the surface.

But she had a feeling that going back to civilization in just a few more hours, that seeing him off to his world and her to hers would leave a far bigger ripple on *her* surface, for a good long time.

"Damn it," she whispered again, but there was no one to hear. She packed up and began to put out the fire, but Michelle got stung by a bee, which freaked her out, and Rock said he'd handle the fire while Lily doctored her wound.

So Lily had her back to the pit, head bent over Michelle's stung leg, when Rose screamed. She whipped around in time to see the fire flare up hot and fast, and Rock fall backwards to his butt in the dirt.

And everything within Lily began to relive her nightmares. "That wasn't water," Rose cried to Rock. "It was the leftover whiskey!"

Lily began running toward the fire, but Rock reached for the second water jug, and tossed that on the flames.

And they burst into a roar and raced toward the sky.

"That was more whiskey!" Rose screamed, and covered her ears, as if standing there on the edge of a now out-of-control campfire with her hands over her ears was somehow going to produce a miracle and shut the fire down.

Lily skidded to a halt, transported back in time to waking up surrounded by flames licking at her legs, her arms, and, in a mindless panic, backing herself right off the edge of a cliff.

She'd made a mistake then, a bad one...and remembering it, she blinked, forced her mind on the here and now as she rushed forward to push Rose back. In her peripheral vision she could see Jared running towards her, but she didn't need saving, not this time. "Stay back," she yelled to Rock, who'd come up to his knees. Grabbing her folding shovel out of her pack, she began tossing dirt onto the fire, working hard and fast on the stubborn flames until they reluctantly subsided.

At her sides now were Jared and Rock, doing what

they could to kick more dirt into the pit, none of them giving up until the flames had been controlled and subdued.

"My God," Michelle finally said as they sagged back, dirty and sweaty. "That could have gone all bad." She looked at Lily with admiration. "Man, you're good."

Lily swiped her drenched forehead and let out a laugh.

"I'm sorry," Rock said, sounding shaken. "God, I nearly started a forest fire."

"Accidents happen," Jared said, and looked at Lily.

Yeah. Yeah, they did. And people either learned and grew, or they didn't.

She'd like to think she'd done the learning-and-growing thing. "It's okay," she said, knowing it was true. They were okay, she was okay. She smiled at Jared, wondering if he could see it all over her face.

But though he smiled back, it didn't quite reach his eyes, and whatever he read in her face, he turned away.

Yeah, maybe she hadn't made a mistake with the fire this time, but there were still some areas in which her mistakes hadn't quite been rectified.

"Do you miss firefighting?" Rose asked.

"I did." She glanced at Jared's back. "But now? I'm good doing this."

Jared walked away, and her heart fell to her toes. "Really good," she whispered, but he didn't stop.

He just kept going.

THE END of their trip was shockingly anticlimatic. Back at the trailhead, Lily called Keith to check in.

"Hey, Lil." He sounded warm as ever, and happy to

hear from her. "So…did you find what you were looking for out there?"

She looked at Jack and Michelle, driving off into the peach-and-gold sunset, happy in their rediscovered passion, secure in the knowledge that they were together for the right reasons—and unable to take their hands off each other. With or without daddy's money, it didn't matter; they were going to make it. "I'm thinking I got closer," she said.

"I'm glad," Keith said, sounding as though he really meant it. "Want me to book you on some more trips? You up for it?"

She'd been so unsure that she could do this. Her faith in everything had been shaken to the core, but in the end, she'd conquered her own fears, she'd done something right. She'd found her strength. "Yes," she said. "Book me."

ROSE DIDN'T dawdle much. She spent a moment putting her gear in order, then blew a kiss to Rock. She'd figured he'd get into his car and drive off into the sunset.

That's what she wanted him to do, so there wouldn't be any lengthy good-bye.

She hated good-byes. It was why she never made them.

But he didn't get into his car, he stepped close and stopped her from getting into the taxi she'd paid to have waiting for her.

"Wait," he murmured. "Hold up a second."

Pretending that was just fine, Rose smiled up at him. "One more kiss, sugar? Is that what you're needing?"

"Truthfully?" Rock rubbed his jaw, his four-day-old growth rasping in the silence. "I'd like more than a kiss."

Rose raised an eyebrow. "Name it."

"I'd like a date."

"A date," she repeated slowly, the concept utterly alien. She didn't date men. She inhaled them, then spat them back out and moved on.

He just smiled. "You. Me. A restaurant, dancing, candles, wine, the whole shebang. What do you say?"

"I'd say you don't have to go to that much trouble, cowboy. You've already had me."

Rock shook his head. "I'm not trying to get laid, Rose."

"Well, that's a shame."

He looked a little exasperated. "I'm trying to get…*more.*"

Rose blinked. "More. From me."

Rock lifted her hand and brought her fingers to his mouth. "That's right."

"I'm twelve years older than you," she reminded him.

"That's my favorite part."

She eyed him for a long moment, not quite sure why hope suddenly bubbled in her throat, cutting off her air supply. "I offered you a deal no man could refuse. A string-free affair. You're a fool to want more."

"Then call me a fool. Say yes, Rose."

She looked him over good. She saw sincerity and something else, something new…affection. Oh, God, she liked the look of that.

He was waiting patiently, and she found herself lifting a casual shoulder even though she felt anything but casual. "Okay, what the hell."

"Is that a yes?"

"Yes, it's a yes. It's a hell, yes," she said with a baffled laugh. "I'll go on a fancy date with you." She shook her head. "We're crazy, you know that?"

"Certifiably nuts, the both of us," Rock agreed, and pulled her close.

AND THEN it was just Lily.

Oh, and Jared.

Only he wasn't smiling, but looking at her. Through her.

Into her.

"Good-bye," she said, her heart snagging on the words. "I know you probably won't believe this, but I'll never forget you."

"Lily—"

"Please don't drag this out," she whispered, suddenly unable to talk past the lump the size of a river rock stuck in her throat. "We knew each other for four days. The end."

"Do you believe in chance, Lily?"

"Jared—"

"Do you?"

"Yes. Damn it, you know I do."

"I came here on a *chance,* because of a list." He pulled the folded paper out of his pocket to remind her. "Things happen, Lily. We happened."

"I didn't plan on this."

"And a year ago I thought my life was all planned out, too. Go with the flow, Lily."

"Jared…"

"Look, life isn't set, Lily. And you know what? I'm thinking that it isn't supposed to be. There's no topo map, and I'm starting to see that's the amazement of the whole thing. *Nothing's* set. You adjust for the things that come up: jobs, adventures. Cancer." He stepped closer. "Love."

Oh, God.

He laughed softly, utterly without mirth, and unfolded his list. "But none of that matters when it's not meant to be." Reaching into his car, he grabbed a pen, then crossed off *One, take a guided trek in the mountains.* "There." He slipped the paper back into his pocket. Looking at her again, he touched her jaw. "Thanks for an unforgettable four days, Lily. I won't forget you, either."

And then he got into his car, and without a backwards glance, drove off into the sunset.

She stared at the dust that rose from his tires. She'd gotten what she wanted.

So why didn't it seem like it?

JARED WENT BACK to work, with some qualms. Once work had been how he defined himself, but he refused to let it come to that ever again. Work was work, not his life.

Knowing that, he was careful to jump back in slowly, forcing himself to leave the office by five o'clock so that he could still have a social life. That his social life consisted mostly of his family was something Candace bitched about, but he held firm. But then, after three weeks, he gave into his assistant's nagging and went on a blind date.

The woman was lovely and smart and attractive, but not Lily, and he figured it out—he wasn't ready. Instead he decided to knock something else off his list—a sail through the Greek Islands. He was leaving the following week, and had a shitload of work to do before then.

Candace poked her head into his office. "Hey. Someone's here to see you."

He pushed up his glasses and looked at his schedule. No meetings. "Who?"

She lifted a shoulder. "Don't know, but I'm leaving for lunch."

He took a glance at the clock on his office wall. "It's ten o'clock."

"Yeah, but my stomach says it's Micky D time. What's your order? Oh, wait, you're giving up Micky D to eat more fish." She grinned. "Sorry, boss. Be back in an hour."

"An hour?" But she was already gone, and he was talking to himself. He had no idea who was waiting to see him, maybe his mother, or any one of his sisters, all of whom had taken to stopping by at least weekly just to look at him.

It'd been comforting. At first. But ever since he'd gotten back from the Sierras, a truly life-altering event, when they'd taken one look at him and known something had happened to him, it was no longer comforting at all. They wanted to know what was wrong, what had happened to him out there, and he hadn't been able to talk about it yet, to tell them the truth.

Once, his body had failed him, but he'd managed a comeback. His heart had been left untouched.

Not this time. Now he was trying to heal that in the same manner he had his body, with sheer will.

So why did he still feel as if he was holding on by a damn string?

Three weeks…

Get over it, Skye, it's past time to get over it. He stood up, but before he could walk around his desk, another head poked in his office. Not Candace, coming back to bug him about a lunch order. Not his mother, or any of his four sisters.

Lily.

She smiled a little shakily, clearly unsure of her welcome. "Hi."

Flummoxed, he just stood there.

"Um, is it a bad time?"

Well that depended on whether she minded watching him try like hell to find his tongue. She wore a gauzy sundress that showed off her tanned shoulders and toned arms. It hugged her breasts, flared out at her hips, and revealed the legs he'd loved having wrapped around him more than anything else in the world.

"I probably should have called." Biting her lower lip, she came all the way into his office. "But I wasn't sure you'd want to see me."

Was she kidding? He couldn't tear his eyes off her. Hell, yeah, he wanted to see her. He wanted never to stop seeing her.

She shot him a smile that he realized with a shock was filled with nerves. She clasped her hands. "I missed you."

Yeah, probably he should have his hearing checked. Because it sounded like she'd said she missed him…

"I know that sounds ridiculous, given how it all ended so badly, but…" Spreading her hands out, she stared down at them, then lifted her head, her eyes glittering with emotion, fierce, stark emotion. "I can't stop thinking about you, Jared. About the odds you've overcome, how you had to go through such trauma just to get the kick in the ass you needed to really live your life. See, I want to live my life, too. Without shielding myself or my heart." She nodded, determined. "I'm not going to do that anymore."

For the first time in three weeks, the fist that had gripped Jared's heart loosened enough for him to breathe, really breathe.

"So maybe," she said. "You'd like to spend some time with me? We could start small, like a date… If you're free. Maybe this weekend…or next if you're busy."

He was free. So damn free.

"I really wish you'd say something," she whispered, clasping her fingers together. "Anything."

"Sorry." He found his legs and came around his desk as a fierce exhilaration and overwhelming joy flowed through his veins. "It's just that I can't go out with you next week, I'm leaving for a sail through the Greek Islands."

"Oh," she said in a very small voice.

"But seeing as I missed you, too, so goddamned much, maybe you could stand to take the trip with me?"

She let out a choked laugh that was part sob, and covered her mouth with a shaking hand.

"I haven't stopped thinking about you either," he said, finally able to get it together to talk. "Not for one single second of a single minute since I drove off that mountain without you." He came to a stop right before her and took her hands. "Now you."

"I can barely breathe, much less speak." She entwined their fingers. "I should tell you right here and now, before I kiss you and forget everything else including my name, that I've been thinking about some stuff."

"Me stuff?"

"Yeah, you stuff." She swallowed hard. "The seeing-you stuff. Seeing you a lot." She smiled, and stole his heart all over again. "Look, we both know I've always walked away. It's what I do."

He shook his head. "I had no right to judge you."

"It doesn't matter. I'm tired of starting over, Jared. I don't want a good-bye this time, or an ending. I want…us. You said you loved me," she said. "I thought it was too much too soon, but someone once told me these things can happen in a second." Her eyes filled. "A year. There's no set time." She smiled shakily. "It took me four days and three weeks, but I love you back, Jared."

It was possible his heart was stuck in his throat, because when he opened his mouth nothing came out of it.

"Oh, God, we're back to that you-not-talking thing again." She drew a trembly breath. "Okay. It's all right if you're not ready to do this. I got that."

"No. *Yes,*" he corrected when she whirled for the door. He caught her, barely, and turned her back to face him. "I'm ready for this, so ready." He shook his head, trying to absorb it all. "It's just that you showed up here, my single favorite walking/talking fantasy, and smiled at me, and from that second on, I lost my train of thought."

She stared at him, and he had to let out a laugh. "Maybe…maybe you could say it again," he said. "Maybe then it'd sink in."

"Which part?"

"The *L*-word part."

She stared at him, then laughed as a tear escaped. "That must have really thrown you, huh?" She slid her arms up around his neck and pressed close. "I meant it, Jared. I don't know the how or the why of it, you with your gadgets and toys, and me with my wanderlust ways, but I love you."

Tossing his glasses to his desk, he hauled her close. Lifting her up, he spun around. "I am never going to get tired of hearing that." Setting her down, he cupped her face. "Say it again."

She laughed, and it sounded far more free this time. "I love you, Jared Skye."

"Oh, yeah, I could get very used to hearing that."

"And besides the fact that it's getting easier to say…" She slid her body against his suggestively. "It's also a surprising aphrodisiac."

"Is it?"

"Uh-huh." She looked over his shoulder at his desk. "How strong is that thing, do you think?"

Laughing in relief, in joy, in overwhelming love, he backed her to it, then lifted her, setting her down next to his laptop. Putting his hands on her thighs, he opened them, then stepped in between, coming up flush to her body.

Ah, yeah, he'd missed this. So damned much. "Seems strong enough."

She shoved his shirt up and put her lips to the spot right over his heart.

Undone, he held her close. "I'm thinking it's plenty strong enough."

"The desk?"

"You. Me. Us. All of it."

Smiling, she pulled him down with her. "Well, then, what are we waiting for...?"

Epilogue

LILY SAT anxiously in her seat as the airplane taxied into the terminal. She was just coming back from a two-week backpacking trip guiding a private party through the Cascades. It'd been a wonderful, successful trek, her fourth since she'd begun working for Keith again, but all she could think about was getting back to Jared.

She'd missed him.

There would be no more trips for a while now, because she was going to be extremely busy for the next few months.

A wedding did that to a person.

She couldn't wait. Grinning, she went into her backpack for some lip balm, and found the *U.S. Weekly Review* with the "Adrenaline Rush" article. She looked at the dog-eared page she'd read so long ago in her physical therapist's office, the article that had changed her life. She fingered the Post-it note, and smiling, set the entire magazine down on the empty seat next to her. "Time to pass on the good luck, and change someone else's destiny."

With that, she stood and exited the plane, and walked right into Jared's waiting arms.

Experience the anticipation, the thrill of the chase
and the sheer rush of falling in love!
Turn the page for a sneak preview of a new book from
Harlequin Romance
THE REBEL PRINCE by Raye Morgan
On sale August 29th wherever books are sold

———

"OH, NO!"

The reaction slipped out before Emma Valentine could stop it, for there stood the very man she most wanted to avoid seeing again.

He didn't look any happier to see her.

"Well, come on, get on board," he said gruffly. "I won't bite." One eyebrow rose. "Though I might nibble a little," he added, mostly to amuse himself.

But she wasn't paying any attention to what he was saying. She was staring at him, taking in the royal blue uniform he was wearing, with gold braid and glistening badges decorating the sleeves, epaulettes and an upright collar. Ribbons and medals covered the breast of the short, fitted jacket. A gold-encrusted sabre hung at his side. And suddenly it was clear to her who this man really was.

She gulped wordlessly. Reaching out, he took her elbow and pulled her aboard. The doors slid closed. And finally she found her tongue.

"You…you're the prince."

He nodded, barely glancing at her. "Yes. Of course."

She raised a hand and covered her mouth for a moment. "I should have known."

"Of course you should have. I don't know why you didn't." He punched the ground-floor button to get the elevator moving again, then turned to look down at her. "A relatively bright five-year-old child would have tumbled to the truth right away."

Her shock faded as her indignation at his tone asserted itself. He might be the prince, but he was still just as annoying as he had been earlier that day.

"A relatively bright five-year-old child without a bump on the head from a badly thrown water polo ball, maybe," she said defensively. She wasn't feeling woozy any longer and she wasn't about to let him bully her, no matter how royal he was. "I was unconscious half the time."

"And just clueless the other half, I guess," he said, looking bemused.

The arrogance of the man was really galling.

"I suppose you think your 'royalness' is so obvious it sort of shimmers around you for all to see?" she challenged. "Or better yet, oozes from your pores like…like sweat on a hot day?"

"Something like that," he acknowledged calmly. "Most people tumble to it pretty quickly. In fact, it's hard to hide even when I want to avoid dealing with it."

"Poor baby," she said, still resenting his manner. "I guess that works better with injured people who are half asleep." Looking at him, she felt a strange emotion she couldn't identify. It was as though she wanted to prove something to him, but she wasn't sure what. "And anyway, you know you did your best to fool me," she added.

His brows knit together as though he really didn't know what she was talking about. "I didn't do a thing."

"You told me your name was Monty."

"It is." He shrugged. "I have a lot of names. Some of them are too rude to be spoken to my face, I'm sure." He glanced at her sideways, his hand on the hilt of his sabre. "Perhaps you're contemplating one of those right now."

You bet I am.

That was what she would like to say. But it suddenly occurred to her that she was supposed to be working for this man. If she wanted to keep the job of coronation chef, maybe she'd better keep her opinions to herself. So she clamped her mouth shut, took a deep breath and looked away, trying hard to calm down.

The elevator ground to a halt and the doors slid open laboriously. She moved to step forward, hoping to make her escape, but his hand shot out again and caught her elbow.

"Wait a minute. *You're* a woman," he said, as though that thought had just presented itself to him.

"That's a rare ability for insight you have there, Your Highness," she snapped before she could stop herself. And then she winced. She was going to have to do better than that if she was going to keep this relationship on an even keel.

But he was ignoring her dig. Nodding, he stared at her with a speculative gleam in his golden eyes. "I've been looking for a woman, but you'll do."

She blanched, stiffening. "I'll do for what?"

He made a head gesture in a direction she knew was opposite of where she was going and his grip tightened on her elbow.

"Come with me," he said abruptly, making it an order.

She dug in her heels, thinking fast. She didn't much like orders. "Wait! I can't. I have to get to the kitchen."

"Not yet. I need you."

"You what?" Her breathless gasp of surprise was soft, but she knew he'd heard it.

"I need you," he said firmly. "Oh, don't look so shocked. I'm not planning to throw you into the hay and have my way with you. I need you for something a bit more mundane than that."

She felt color rushing into her cheeks and she silently begged it to stop. Here she was, formless and stodgy in her chef's whites. No makeup, no stiletto heels. Hardly the picture of the femmes fatales he was undoubtedly used to. The likelihood that he would have any carnal interest in her was remote at best. To have him think she was hysterically defending her virtue was humiliating.

"Well, what if I don't want to go with you?" she said in hopes of deflecting his attention from her blush.

"Too bad."

"What?"

Amusement sparkled in his eyes. He was certainly enjoying this. And that only made her more determined to resist him.

"I'm the prince, remember? And we're in the castle. My orders take precedence. It's that old pesky divine rights thing."

Her jaw jutted out. Despite her embarrassment, she couldn't let that pass.

"Over my free will? Never!"

Exasperation filled his face.

"Hey, call out the historians. Someone will write a book about you and your courageous principles." His eyes glittered sardonically. "But in the meantime, Emma Valentine, you're coming with me."

SAVE UP TO $30! SIGN UP TODAY!

INSIDE *Romance*

The complete guide to your favorite
Harlequin®, Silhouette® and Love Inspired® books.

✓ Newsletter ABSOLUTELY FREE! No purchase necessary.

✓ Valuable coupons for future purchases of Harlequin,
Silhouette and Love Inspired books in every issue!

✓ Special excerpts & previews in each issue. Learn about all
the hottest titles before they arrive in stores.

✓ No hassle—mailed directly to your door!

✓ Comes complete with a handy shopping checklist
so you won't miss out on any titles.

- -

SIGN ME UP TO RECEIVE INSIDE ROMANCE
ABSOLUTELY FREE
(Please print clearly)

Name

Address

City/Town   State/Province   Zip/Postal Code

(098 KKM EJL9)

Please mail this form to:
In the U.S.A.: Inside Romance, P.O. Box 9057, Buffalo, NY 14269-9057
In Canada: Inside Romance, P.O. Box 622, Fort Erie, ON L2A 5X3
OR visit http://www.eHarlequin.com/insideromance

IRNBPA06R   ® and ™ are trademarks owned and used by the trademark owner and/or its licensee.

Silhouette® Desire®

Introducing an exciting appearance by legendary _New York Times_ bestselling author

DIANA PALMER
HEARTBREAKER

He's the ultimate bachelor…
but he may have just met
the one woman to change his ways!

Join the drama in the story of a confirmed
bachelor, an amnesiac beauty and their
unexpected passionate romance.

"Diana Palmer is a mesmerizing storyteller
who captures the essence of what
a romance should be."—_Affaire de Coeur_

**Heartbreaker _is available from Silhouette Desire_
in September 2006.**

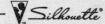

SPECIAL EDITION™

COMING IN SEPTEMBER FROM
USA TODAY BESTSELLING AUTHOR

SUSAN MALLERY

THE LADIES' MAN

Rachel Harper wondered how she'd tell
Carter Brockett the news—their spontaneous
night of passion had left her pregnant!
What would he think of the naive
schoolteacher who'd lost control? After
all, the man had a legion of exes who'd
been unable to snare a commitment, and
here she had a forever-binding one!

Then she remembered.
He'd lost control, too....

positively
+pregnant

Sometimes the unexpected
is the best news of all...